The Spirit of L[...]

Odella started to r[...]
believed the carria[...]er.

She was terrified [...] heard, also
afraid she would nev[...]le to tell the Marquis
about it.

With a sense of relief she saw that the carriage
was there.

The driver must have seen her coming, for he
was waiting with the door open.

As she half-collapsed in the seat, she realised
somebody else was there and she gave a shriek
of terror.

"It is all right," a quiet voice said. "It is only
me."

It was the Marquis!

A Camfield Novel of Love
by Barbara Cartland

———

"Barbara Cartland's novels are all distinguished by their
intelligence, good sense, and good nature...."

—ROMANTIC TIMES

"Who could give better advice on how to keep your romance
going strong than the world's most famous romance novelist, Barbara Cartland?"

—THE STAR

Camfield Place,
Hatfield
Hertfordshire,
England

Dearest Reader,

Camfield Novels of Love mark a very exciting era of my books with Jove. They have already published nearly two hundred of my titles since they became my first publisher in America, and now all my original paperback romances in the future will be published exclusively by them.

As you already know, Camfield Place in Hertfordshire is my home, which originally existed in 1275, but was rebuilt in 1867 by the grandfather of Beatrix Potter.

It was here in this lovely house, with the best view in the county, that she wrote *The Tale of Peter Rabbit*. Mr. McGregor's garden is exactly as she described it. The door in the wall that the fat little rabbit could not squeeze underneath and the goldfish pool where the white cat sat twitching its tail are still there.

I had Camfield Place blessed when I came here in 1950 and was so happy with my husband until he died, and now with my children and grandchildren, that I know the atmosphere is filled with love and we have all been very lucky.

It is easy here to write of love and I know you will enjoy the Camfield Novels of Love. Their plots are definitely exciting and the covers very romantic. They come to you, like all my books, with love.

Bless you,

Barbara Cartland

CAMFIELD NOVELS OF LOVE
by Barbara Cartland

A NEW CAMFIELD NOVEL OF LOVE BY

BARBARA CARTLAND

The Spirit of Love

JOVE BOOKS, NEW YORK

THE SPIRIT OF LOVE

A Jove Book / published by arrangement with
the author

PRINTING HISTORY
Jove edition / October 1994

All rights reserved.
Copyright © 1994 by Barbara Cartland.
Cover art copyright © 1994 by Fiord Forlag A/S.
This book may not be reproduced in whole
or in part, by mimeograph or any other means,
without permission. For information address:
The Berkley Publishing Group, 200 Madison Avenue,
New York, New York 10016.

ISBN: 0-515-11479-0

A JOVE BOOK®
Jove Books are published by The Berkley Publishing Group,
200 Madison Avenue, New York, New York 10016.
JOVE and the "J" design are trademarks
belonging to Jove Publications, Inc.

PRINTED IN THE UNITED STATES OF AMERICA

10 9 8 7 6 5 4 3 2 1

Author's Note

THIS is my 500th book and I have chosen for it my favourite period—the Regency.

I owe dozens of plots for my books to my dear friend, the late Sir Arthur Bryant. He used to laugh when I told him that I plagiarized his brilliant books and say that he was delighted for me to do so.

I owe so much to *The Years of Endurance 1773–1802*, *The Years of Victory 1802–1812*, and *The Age of Elegance 1812–1822*.

When Sir Arthur gave me his last book, *Spirit of England*, he inscribed it:

To Barbara
Who understands so well.
With the
affection and admiration
of the Author.

I must therefore dedicate this, my 500th book,
The Spirit of Love

To Sir Arthur Bryant
one of our greatest Historians
whose books
fascinating, human, and inspiring
will live forever in the hearts
of those
who love ENGLAND

chapter one

1814

As the open carriage turned into a road where a great number of people were moving about, there was the sound of music in the distance.

Odella Wayne, who was sitting on the back seat, bent forward to see if she could discern where the music was coming from.

When she saw what was happening and that people were moving hastily to clear the road, she gave an exclamation.

"It is a Circus!"

The maid, who was sitting opposite, exclaimed:

"Miss Odella, how excitin'!"

The coachman, an elderly man who had driven the Rector for many years, pulled the horse to one side.

"Us'll 'ave t' wait 'ere, Miss Odella," he said over

his shoulder, " 'till they passes."

"That is a good idea, Thompson," Odella replied, "and it will give us an excellent view of them."

She realised that Emily, the maid, was straining to see what she could over her shoulder.

"Come and sit beside me, Emily," she said kindly. "You will have a better view from this seat."

"Oh, thank you, Miss Odella," Emily answered. "Oi've always been mad about th' Circus ever since Oi' were a child."

Odella smiled, knowing that was not so many years ago.

When she had decided, since Father was away from home, to go shopping in Portsmouth, she ordered the carriage in which he usually travelled.

She suggested to the Housekeeper, Mrs. Barnet, that she should come with her, but the elderly woman replied:

"I 'ave to refuse, Miss Odella. I've got too much to do. When th' Master's away, it's my one chance of gettin' 'is Study cleaned. You know 'ow he goes on if we disturb 'is books when 'e's at 'ome."

Odella smiled.

"I am sure you are right to take the opportunity," she agreed. "Papa does get very upset if we move his books, especially those he is using for his research."

The Rector was writing a history of the village of Nettleway, which was his Parish.

As he required a lot of books for reference, they were piled up on every table in the Study and on the floor.

She could understand Mrs. Barnet's desire to get things clean while she had the chance.

"There are some things I want in Portsmouth," Odella said, "so I will take Emily with me. I know Papa would not like me to go alone."

"I should think not indeed!" Mrs. Barnet declared as though Odella had suggested something improper. "And your Mother, God rest her soul, would never have let you go into the town on your own."

That was certainly true because Portsmouth at the moment was very different from the Portsmouth of old, before the war.

Now the tide seemed to have turned against Napoleon, and every day Wellington was sending home encouraging reports of progress.

People were very much more cheerful than they had been the previous year.

Last Spring and Summer the roads to Portsmouth and Plymouth had been filled with troops.

There were the jangling Household Cavalry with splendid accoutrements on excellent horses who were to travel with them.

There were Reserve Battalions marching to reinforce their Regiments, who were by now veterans of the Peninsular War and detachments of rosy-cheeked militiamen under raw young Ensigns "in fine new toggery."

They came through the villages, their drums and fifes playing, with little boys running excitedly behind them.

The housewives rushed to their cottage-doors and windows to see them pass.

The older women mourned over the "young lambs going to the slaughter."

The older men and those who had returned

3

wounded to England muttered that they did not know what was "a-coming to 'em."

Odella and her Father often talked of the carnage awaiting them after they had crossed the bay.

She wondered what the soldiers would think when they saw for the first time the barren, tawny shores of the Peninsula.

The men who returned would come to tell the Rector of their experiences, feeling he was the one person in the village who would understand.

They would describe all too vividly the stink of Lisbon and what they felt as they marched out of the Belem barracks on the long mountain track, to the frontier between Portugal and Spain.

Some of the stories they told had made Odella want to cry, others were very funny.

One young man who had returned home only slightly wounded was the Doctor's son, Tim Howland.

He described vividly to the Rector, whom he had known since he was a child, what he and the men with him had experienced.

Bug-bitten, footsore, and dusty they had finally found themselves among the tattered, cheery veterans who were to be their comrades.

"It was then our education began," Tim said.

The Rector raised his eye-brows and he explained:

"I and a large number of others were taken by Major O'Hara of the Rifles to where we could look down from a rocky height at the enemy on the plain below.

" 'Those are the French,' he barked in his barrack-yard voice. 'You must kill those fellows, and not allow them to kill you. You must learn

4

to do as these old birds do, and get cover where you can. Remember, recruits, you have come here to kill, not to be killed. Bear this in mind; if you do not kill the French, they will kill you.' "

"That was certainly plain-speaking," the Rector remarked.

"That is what we thought," Tim replied. "And it was true enough, as we were to find out for ourselves."

After what she had heard, Odella had always prayed for each consignment as it arrived.

Marching behind the drums and fifes, the soldiers obviously enjoyed the cheers of the crowd.

They appreciated the young girls who ran out to thrust flowers into their hands, or give them kisses.

She wondered how many would return, and how many would be buried in unmarked graves.

In the beginning of his great offensive in May 1813, Wellington had under his command more than 50,000 British troops and nearly 30,000 Portuguese.

Now, by the following February, Wellington had a firm foothold across the Pyrenees in the Southwest of France, and the people of Spain had become friends.

"Oh, Miss, oh, do look!" Emily cried.

As the music grew louder, it was certainly not the fifes and drums Odella had heard so often.

She leant over her side of the carriage to look up the road.

She was not surprised that Emily was excited.

There was a colourful parade coming down the street towards them.

It was led by a man wearing a red coat and black top-hat, which he raised every so often to the women waving to him.

He was riding a fine black horse.

Behind him there were four other horses ridden by pretty young women wearing ballet skirts which revealed their shapely legs.

They wore on their heads glittering crowns, fluttering feathers, and what looked like flashing jewels.

Emily was so excited that she got off the seat beside Odella.

Kneeling on the opposite seat, which had its back to the horses, she could see better without obscuring her mistress's view.

Nearer and nearer they came.

Now Odella could see that the Band was being carried on a wagon drawn by two white horses.

They were driven by a man wearing the skin and head of a tiger.

Cymbals were being clashed to make the loudest noise possible, and the big drum boomed out to the delight of the crowd.

The Bandsmen were all dressed in fairy costumes.

This wagon was followed by some clowns who cracked jokes with the passers-by, and waved balloons on sticks in front of the children.

They whisked them away, however, before the boys could catch them.

With their white faces, exaggerated red lips, and strange pantaloons, it was impossible not to laugh at them.

Every movement they made and every word they said brought peals of laughter from those they were passing.

On another wagon, covered, not like the others in scarlet, but in glittering silver, came a spectacular figure.

Seated on what appeared to be a throne, she was dressed in a shimmering gown which caught the sun's rays and glittered with every movement.

It covered not only her body, but also her head.

She wore over her face what Odella recognised as a *yashmak*.

Her eyes were revealed, but beneath them there was a veil of rose-pink gauze.

In one hand she held a large crystal ball, in the other a pack of cards.

"She be th' Fortune-Teller, Miss Odella!" Emily gasped. "Oi've 'eard 'bout 'er!"

Odella thought she certainly looked the part.

Then, just as they reached a point on the road from which they were watching, the man in the red coat called a halt.

He drew in his horse, as did those behind him, and the two wagons came to a standstill.

"Ladies and Gentlemen!" he called out in a voice which seemed to echo round the houses and hushed the crowds into silence. "Friends of Portsmouth! This afternoon, at three o'clock, there will be a performance of the Circus in Lincoln Field, and another at six. Come and join us! Come and see the brilliance of our Ballerinas on horseback—the way our clowns can make you laugh—and consult *Madame* Zosina, who will tell you what wonderful surprises await you in the future!"

He paused to say even more impressively:

"Because we all wish 'Good Luck' to the brave men who are fighting for us against Napoleon,

Madame Zosina will tell the future of every Serviceman for half the price she charges to the rest of us."

There were loud cheers at this.

Madame Zosina bent her head in acknowledgement, first to one side of the street, then the other.

"Three o'clock!" the Ringmaster shouted. "And do not be late!"

Then the Band struck up and they were off again, the people waving to them on the pavements and from the windows.

They were accompanied by a crowd of small boys running excitedly beside the horses and the wagons.

As they disappeared, Emily gave a deep sigh.

"That were lovely, Miss Odella!" she said. "Oi'd love t'have me fortune told."

She looked pleadingly at Odella as she spoke.

Because Odella was fond of the girl, who was only just seventeen and a year younger than herself, she said:

"If we get our shopping done quickly, perhaps we can go to the Circus."

Emily clasped her hands together.

"Oh, Miss Odella, d'you mean that? It'll be somethin' Oi'll remember all me life!"

"I hope you will have a great deal more than that to remember," Odella replied. "As we do not have to hurry home to give my Father his tea, we will go to the Circus, but we must finish our shopping first."

The carriage was already moving and Thompson turned at the far end of the street.

Odella had made a list of the things that were wanted both by Mrs. Barnet, who was short of cleaning materials, and by Betsy the Cook.

Betsy had been at the Rectory for many years and was always complaining that the local shops did not stock the ingredients she wanted.

It was an old complaint which Odella had heard a hundred times.

She had therefore brought with her now a list of exactly what Betsy wanted.

Although it took time, they managed to purchase almost everything they required before it was a quarter to three.

Odella was well aware that while she was asking for first one thing, then another, Emily was watching the clock.

She was desperately afraid that if they were late they would not be able to get a seat.

Odella thought, however, that it was unlikely that the Circus would be full in the afternoon.

It was in the evening, when the shops were closed and people had nothing else to do, that they would flock to Lincoln Field, where the Circus had been set up.

Then every seat would be taken.

When finally Odella told Thompson where to take them, Emily was almost jumping for joy.

"Now, what do you want to do, Emily?" Odella asked. "Shall we go into the 'Big Top' and watch the clowns, the horses, and I expect there will be monkeys, too, or do you want to visit *Madame Zosina*?"

Emily thought it over and, as she was not very quick-witted, it took her some time.

"Oi' thinks, Miss Odella," she replied at last, "we should go t' *Madame* Zosina first. There won't be many people waiting to see her early in th' afternoon, and later 'er might leave afore we gets to 'er."

Odella laughed, thinking it was good reasoning on Emily's part.

"Very well," she said, "*Madame* Zosina first."

When they arrived at the field it was easy to see *Madame*'s tent.

It stood away from the others by itself, and instead of being like the other tents, it was red with her name emblazoned on it in gold.

Outside the tent there were two large palm trees, each standing in a tub.

Odella purchased their tickets and she and Emily went inside.

There was a row of chairs on either side of the tent for those who were waiting to go into the inner sanctum.

Madame Zosina was hidden from their gaze by a glittering curtain rather like the gown she wore and the veil which covered her hair.

Odella realised how everything was designed to excite the imagination and anticipation of those who consulted the Fortune-Teller.

There were two sailors waiting to have their fortunes told.

Almost as soon as Odella and Emily had sat down, another sailor came out through the glittering curtain.

He went up to those who were waiting.

As the nearest one jumped up to take his place behind the curtain, he said to him:

" 'Er be marvellous! That's wot she be, an' ye'll be proud t'know me afore Oi'm very much older!"

The man to whom he was speaking disappeared through the glittering curtain.

His friend, who was left behind, laughed.

"If 'er's told ye ye're goin' t'be an Admiral, well, ye shouldn't believe all ye hears!"

"Ye'll be surprised," the young man retorted.

Then he walked jauntily out of the tent into the sunshine.

The sailor he had just been talking to moved up nearer to the curtain.

In case someone came and "stole a march" on them, Odella moved into the seat next to him, and Emily moved up beside her.

They had only just done so, when three girls came into the tent and hastily took chairs on the other side.

"We're goin' t'have t'wait," one of the girls whispered.

" 'T'll be worth it to know th' future," another girl replied. "Oi wants t'know if Bert's serious or not. 'E talks a lot, but 'e don' say wot Oi wants t'hear."

Odella smiled to herself.

She thought it was not very difficult to tell the fortunes of the village girls, which was something she had quite often done herself.

Ever since she had been a child, she had somehow known things about people without being told.

She had been a "Fortune-Teller" for her Father at the Bazaar they held every Summer for the Church, and again when they wanted to raise money for the festivities at Christmas.

The village people thought she was brilliant at her fortune-telling and believed every word she told them.

Her Mother had warned her always to be very careful and not raise false hopes.

"I know, Darling, that you sometimes 'see' things that other people cannot see, and that is a gift from God. But you must not abuse it. You must not promise things that cannot be fulfilled, for people who do not get what they are wishing for can be very unhappy."

Odella had understood.

She had therefore always been very ambiguous in her fortune-telling.

Unless she was absolutely convinced that what she said would actually happen, she did not raise the person's hopes.

It had been difficult since the scale of the war had increased.

Almost every cottage in the village had someone fighting on the Peninsula.

Although she had never revealed it, she had somehow been aware of the deaths of several young men.

Long before their relatives had been informed, Odella knew that they had died in the service of their country.

But she had on two occasions been quite certain that a man would return after his family had given him up for lost.

She had been proved right when one had arrived back wounded, and the other was blind.

She thought now that it would be interesting to see exactly how *Madame* Zosina treated her clients.

She wanted to find out if she was a genuine Fortune-Teller, or only somebody acting the part.

It was usual when any Circus visited Portsmouth or Gosport that there would be a Fortune-Teller among the entertainers.

But from all she had heard, Odella was certain that most of them were not genuine.

They merely preyed on the human frailty of wanting to know the future before it actually happened.

The second sailor seemed to be with *Madame* Zosina for quite a long time.

When he came out he was beaming.

"Ye 'ave a go, Joe," he said to his friend. "Oi'll wait for ye outside."

As he went out smiling, Joe went through the glittering curtain and Odella moved up another seat.

Now she could hear faintly, but none the less clearly what was being said.

"Good-day, Sailor," a soft voice greeted him.

"G'day, Ma'am," the sailor replied. "Me friends 'ave bin tellin' me 'ow good ye be, an' Oi wants to 'ear wot's goin' t'appen to me."

"I expect you are going abroad," *Madame* Zosina said again very softly. "You are eager to know what will happen to you when you reach your destination."

"That be right," Joe agreed.

There was silence.

Odella guessed that as he sat in front of her *Madame* Zosina was gazing into her crystal ball.

She was proved right, when after a few seconds *Madame* said:

"I see you travelling in a big ship, and I think you are going to France."

Joe must have nodded an affirmative, and she went on:

"You have to say good-bye to a lovely young lady."

"That's right," Joe confirmed. "Will 'er be faithful t'me while Oi'm away?"

"I know she will," Zosina replied, "but I think you are unhappy at leaving her."

Joe murmured something that Odella could not hear, and *Madame* Zosina went on:

"You have not very long to tell her how much you love her. You are leaving sooner than you expected."

There was silence before she added:

"Now, let me see—is it three days, or four before you sail?"

" 'Tis three," Joe said eagerly.

"Then you must tell her to-night that you love her and every night until you go. And now—let me look in my crystal—your ship is very large— if I can make out its name I will give you a special talisman to keep you safe wherever you are going."

"Thank ye, Ma'am," Joe said. "Oi'd like that."

"It is, in fact, very, very lucky," Zosina said, "but I must first find the name of your ship."

There was silence until Joe said:

"We be told to tell no-one th' name o' our ship."

"I can understand that," Zosina said quickly. "But I see it clearly in my crystal ball. Now, let me think—"

She must, Odella thought, be peering into her crystal ball.

After a minute she said:

"I see an 'L,' or is it an 'I'?"

"An 'I,' " Joe said quickly.

"Now I see another letter that looks to me like an 'M.' "

"That be an 'N,' " Joe agreed.

"Am I wrong, or is the word *INVINCIBLE*?" *Madame* Zosina asked.

"Ye be right," Joe said, "an' that be real clever o' ye."

"Very well. Here is your talisman and next Wednesday, or is it Thursday, you sail?"

"Oi' thinks it be Wednesday night, Ma'am."

"Then on Wednesday I will think of you and make sure you arrive safely."

"Thank ye, thank ye very much," Joe said.

"I will make sure, too, that your girl thinks of you," *Madame* said. "It is important she should not forget you while you are away."

"Oi be grateful, very grateful," Joe said.

There was the sound of a chair being pushed back, then Joe came through the curtains.

As he did so, Odella realised that a man wearing a soldier's uniform was standing beside her.

"Could I ask ye," he said, "if ye'd let me go in to see the Fortune-Teller afore ye? We've bin told t'be back in barracks by four o'clock an' Oi dare not be late."

"Yes, of course," Odella agreed. "I am in no hurry."

"Thank ye."

The soldier disappeared through the glittering curtain.

Listening, Odella heard *Madame* Zosina talk to

him in very much the same soft, gentle way she had talked to Joe.

She managed at the same time to extract from him the information that he was leaving the day after to-morrow, just as she had done with Joe.

She found out the name of his ship and also the Regiments that were sailing with him.

It was so cleverly done that Odella could hardly believe what she was hearing.

Yet without his realising it, she had made the soldier tell her everything she wanted to know.

As Odella felt the horror of what was happening, she thought it could not be true.

There had been talk all through the war of spies who had infiltrated into England with the smugglers.

Men and women had been bribed into betraying secrets which would be of use to Napoleon.

Her Father had said often enough that it was dangerous to chatter to strangers, however innocent they might appear.

"Because we live near Portsmouth," he had said, "we have to be more careful than anyone else. A careless word could alert the enemy that a ship is leaving. Then they are waiting to attack it as soon as it puts out to sea."

It had, however, never occurred to Odella that men who were sworn to secrecy could be beguiled into revealing information to women like *Madame* Zosina.

Their unguarded words had resulted in their ships being sunk and many lives being lost.

Now she heard *Madame* Zosina giving the soldier a talisman and assuring him that through her magic powers he would be safe.

Odella wanted to scream out that the woman was a spy and a danger.

Then she knew that she would have to be very careful and discreet about what she had heard.

She was quite certain that if *Madame* Zosina became aware that anyone was suspicious of her, she would quickly disappear, or else take some action that could be extremely unpleasant for anyone who denounced her.

When the soldier reappeared through the curtain, Odella told Emily to go in first.

"Oh, no, Miss Odella. 'Tis your turn next!" Emily insisted.

"I have a headache," Odella said. "You go in, and if it is still bad, I can come back another day."

"Oi'm real sorry, Miss Odella," Emily said.

However, she quickly hurried past her to where *Madame* Zosina was waiting.

Listening to what was said, Odella was aware that it was very different from what she had listened to before.

Emily was promised that a tall, handsome man would fall in love with her before the end of the year.

But she would have to be very careful about another man who was unpleasant and should be avoided, or he would make trouble.

"You will receive a message from Overseas which will please you," *Madame* Zosina went on.

"That'll be me brother," Emily said quickly.

"I think you will be seeing him sooner than you expect," the Fortune-Teller finished.

"Well, that be good news, very good news!" Emily replied.

When she came out, she was beaming at what she had heard.

But to her surprise, Odella hurried her out of the tent and into the sunshine.

"I must go home," she said.

"Be yer 'ead very bad, Miss Odella?" Emily asked. "P'raps *Madame* Zosina could have done something fer ye. Her's magic, she is!"

"I am sure she is," Odella agreed.

They walked across the field to where Thompson had parked the carriage under the shade of some trees.

As they got into it, Odella had an idea.

"I have to see the Lord Lieutenant, the Earl of Portsmouth," she said. "We will call there on our way home."

"Very good, Miss Odella," Thompson replied, "but it be a mile or so out o' our way."

"There is no hurry," Odella said, "and I am sure His Lordship will not keep me long."

Thompson drove the carriage slowly over the rough ground and out onto the road.

There were a number of people making their way to the "Big Top."

"Oh, Miss Odella, we be missin' th' Circus!" Emily wailed.

"Perhaps we will be able to come again before the end of the week," Odella said. "I am sorry, Emily, but I do not want to sit in a hot, stuffy tent at the moment."

"Oi understands, Miss, but Oi' did want to see them clowns."

"We will try and come to-morrow, or the day after," Odella replied, "and after all, you have seen *Madame* Zosina."

" 'Er be magic!" Emily said. "There be no other word fer it, Miss Odella, real *Magic*!"

Odella did not reply.

She was thinking that Zosina's magic was dangerous, very dangerous indeed.

The sooner she did something about it, the better.

chapter two

THE Marquis of Midhurst drove down Piccadilly,
aware that all the passers by were looking at his
horses.

He was particularly proud of the pair he was
driving which he had bought two weeks previously
at Tattersalls Salesrooms.

He was astonished when he first saw them
because he could not imagine anyone who
possessed such magnificent horseflesh would be
willing to part with them.

When he learned that their owner had died, he
understood.

They had come from the North, and there were
a number of other bidders when the sale started.

However, they were knocked down to the

Marquis and he was delighted to be the possessor of them.

He found they had been extremely well trained.

When they were attached to his new Phaeton, which was yellow with black wheels and shafts, he knew they made a spectacle that was outstanding.

He turned down St. James's Street and hoped that some of his friends would see him pass from the window of Whites Club.

He thought that after he had seen the Prime Minister he would go back to the Club and hear their comments on his new possession.

What had given him particular pleasure when he had inherited his Father's title and vast estates was that he could now buy horses that would out-pace any others on the race-course.

It went without saying that he was himself an outstanding rider and had been victorious in a number of Steeple-Chases.

But there was a penalty for everything.

He had on his Father's death to leave the Army, and this had taken away some of the glitter from the possessions he had inherited.

He had been wounded in Spain while serving with Wellington's Army and sent back to England to recover.

As he reached Portsmouth despite Napoleon's ships, which were out to sink everything that was in the Bay of Biscay, the 3rd Marquess of Midhurst died.

His son was then informed that he must not rejoin his Regiment.

The Senior Officers at the War Office and the Prince Regent himself explained that if a nobleman of his importance was taken prisoner, or killed, it would be a triumph for Napoleon Bonaparte, who was definitely in need of such.

The Marquis had been angry because he enjoyed being a soldier.

He loved his Regiment and had already received two awards for gallantry.

He knew, however, that the Senior Officers and the Prince Regent were talking sense.

Therefore he said to himself that it was no use "kicking against the pricks."

'Perhaps I can serve my country in some other way,' he thought.

So far, however, he had not been asked to do anything and instead concentrated on enjoying himself.

This was not difficult, considering that he was very handsome, besides being of social importance and extremely rich.

There was not a woman in London who did not dream of attracting the Marquis's attention.

Every woman certainly made every effort to do so.

In fact, as one of the Marquis's contemporaries said:

"The trouble with you, Midhurst, is that as soon as you enter a room, the tempo rises. How can we poor 'also-rans' compete with that?"

The Marquis laughed.

At the same time, he was aware that he had a wide field to choose from.

He would have been inhuman if he had not enjoyed picking out the prettiest and most attractive women who fluttered their eye-lashes at him.

He was very involved at the moment with one of the most exciting women he had ever met.

Lady Georgina Langford was a recognised Beauty at twenty-seven, and had been the toast of St. James's for years.

She did not seem likely to relinquish her leading rôle, and the fact that she was known as the "Tigress" was certainly justified.

The Marquis, with all his experience of women, had never met a woman more passionate, or more insatiable.

Lady Georgina had eloped when she was only eighteen with Walter Langford, who had little to recommend him except a handsome face.

He was known in all the Clubs as a gambler.

He had pursued a number of women before he persuaded the Duke of Cumbria's daughter to run away with him.

The Duke was furious.

Lady Georgina had been married at the May Fair Chapel, where the Parson asked no questions and required no credentials from those he married.

The ceremony was nevertheless legal.

There was nothing the Duke could do, and Walter enjoyed being his son-in-law.

His Grace, however, held tightly on to the purse-strings.

Langford, therefore, made no trouble when his wife accepted expensive presents from her admirers.

There were jewels, furs, and other gifts he could not possibly have afforded himself.

To everybody's surprise, the marriage seemed to be a happy one.

There were no scenes or reproaches when Lady Georgina was engaged with her latest conquest.

There were fortunately no children of the marriage.

The Langfords managed to live in a style which could not have been financed by Walter's success at the card-tables.

From the Marquis's point of view, the fact that Walter was not jealous of him, and Georgina was available when he required her, made things very convenient.

He was thinking as he drove past St. James's Palace that he was to dine with her to-night.

He also intended to take her a present of a bracelet he had seen in Bond Street.

It would certainly embellish the whiteness of her hands, with their long fingers.

He smiled as he thought how she would thank him.

He had already learnt that Walter had gone to Newmarket for the races.

The Marquis turned his horses into Pall Mall and ceased to think of Georgina.

Instead, he was wondering why the Prime Minister wished to see him.

He had met the 2nd Earl of Liverpool on various occasions, but had not been particularly impressed by him.

He had been born Robert Jenkinson and had played a minor part in a number of Governments ever since he had grown up.

At the same time, his handling of the war had not been outstanding.

The Marquis, like many other people, thought wistfully of Pitt, who had died in 1806.

The Marquis moved through Horseguards Parade towards Downing Street.

He was thinking that although the Prime Minister did his best, he was hardly in the class of those Prime Ministers who had made a real impression on the public, or on the enemies of England.

Reaching Downing Street, he drew up his horses with a flourish outside Number 10, and handed the reins to his groom.

As the door was opened to him, he walked in, wondering once again why he had been sent for.

He was told that the Prime Minister was waiting for him in his Sitting-Room.

As he was escorted there, the Marquis wondered if any man at any time had politically had such problems as the Prime Minister of England at that particular moment.

The war had gone on year after year.

Now there was a glimmer of hope that it might end.

It required a very strong man to make sure politically that if we did win the war, we did not lose the peace.

"The Most Honourable Marquis of Midhurst!" the servant who was escorting the Marquis announced as he opened the door to the Sitting-Room.

As the Marquis walked in, he realised that the Prime Minister was not alone.

The Secretary of State for War, the Viscount Castlereagh, was with him.

He was an old friend, and when the Marquis had shaken hands first with the Prime Minister then with the Viscount, he said:

"It is delightful, Castlereagh, to see you again."

"And I have been looking forward to seeing you," the Viscount replied. "Have you recovered completely from your wound?"

"I still limp a little, which infuriates me," the Marquis replied, "but, thank God, I can ride a horse, and I still have two legs."

The Prime Minister and the Viscount both laughed.

They all sat down in comfortable armchairs placed near the fire.

"I have a message for you from Wellington, who has asked in his despatches how you are," the Viscount remarked. "He also told me to tell you that he misses you."

"And I miss him," the Marquis replied. "You know that above all things, I wanted to return to my Regiment."

"We cannot go into all that again!" the Prime Minister said quickly. "We have asked you here, Marquis, because we have a very tricky situation in your County."

The Marquis raised his eye-brows.

"In Hampshire?"

"Exactly!" the Prime Minister replied. "And we thought it was something you could deal with."

The Marquis was curious as to what it could be.

The question that sprang to his mind was answered before it could reach his lips.

"Perhaps you are wondering why we have not approached the Lord Lieutenant?" the Prime Minister said. "The answer is simply that the Earl of Portsmouth is an old man and has indicated that he wished to retire at the end of the year."

"I thought that was what he might do," the Marquis said.

"And of course," the Prime Minister went on, "you will take his place."

The Marquis, who had already assumed this as a foregone conclusion, merely nodded his head.

"Now, the reason we have asked you to come here," the Viscount said, "is that we are desperately worried about the ships that are leaving from Portsmouth."

The Marquis looked surprised.

"I know, of course, that there are a great number of them."

"We have divided the troops we send out to Wellington between Portsmouth and Plymouth," Viscount Castlereagh explained, "but the casualties from Portsmouth are giving us a great deal of anxiety."

"Casualties?" the Marquis queried.

"The ships put to sea at night, as you know," the Viscount continued. "The troops board them at dusk and when they reach the open sea they wait until it is dark before they move farther."

The Marquis, who knew this, nodded his head.

"Every man aboard them," the Viscount went on, "is warned never to divulge to anyone the exact date and time of embarkation."

The Marquis was well aware of this, and so he said nothing.

The Prime Minister spoke next.

"What Castlereagh is trying to say," he said, "is that for the last month the ships leaving Portsmouth have been attacked by French vessels that appear to be lying in wait for them as if they already knew on what date they could expect them."

The Marquis drew in his breath.

"Are you really telling me that there are spies in Portsmouth who are extracting information from the troops, which results in the French Navy knowing exactly when ships carrying troops will leave the harbour?"

"That is what I am trying to say," the Prime Minister agreed, "although it seems almost impossible."

"I suppose nothing is impossible in war!" the Marquis remarked. "But it is difficult to understand how the information obtained through careless talk can be carried so quickly across the Channel to the French Navy—what is left of it!"

He spoke the last words scathingly, and Viscount Castlereagh said quickly:

"It would be a mistake, Midhurst, to underrate their intelligence, especially if it enables them to destroy our Forces before they even have a chance of going into battle under Wellington."

"I agree with you," the Marquis replied, "but what do you suggest should be done about it?"

"That is exactly why we have asked you here," the Prime Minister said. "Portsmouth is in your County. Besides which, if any man can cope with this particular situation, it is yourself!"

"You flatter me," the Marquis replied.

At the same time, he knew that he had on two separate occasions changed a defeat into a victory by being perceptively aware of what the enemy would do next.

"Wellington informed me," Viscount Castlereagh said, "that it was you who had advised him, before you were invalided home, that as soon as he crossed the Pyrenees into France he should foster good-will with the civilian population."

The Marquis did not confirm this.

However, he had worked out that if the English were to retain numerical superiority in the field, they could spare no troops to hold down territory in the rear.

When the mid-Winter rains had bogged down the Armies, Wellington remembered the Marquis's advice about the local population.

He devoted himself to putting it into effect.

In this he was actually helped by the French troops.

After enjoying twenty years of rape, pillage, and arson in all the countries of Europe which they had over-run, they had recently behaved in the same way at home.

Most of the Spaniards had to be sent home because, as Wellington told their Commander, he had not sacrificed thousands to enable the survivors to rob the French.

The British troops included a large number of gaol-birds.

These he treated in his usual realistic way by sending a strong force of Military Police up and down the columns.

They had orders to string up on the spot any man who was found pilfering.

After a few examples, there was no further plundering.

Such a manner of making war astonished the French.

They could scarcely believe their eyes.

An Innkeeper veteran of Napoleon's Italian

campaigns was speechless when Brigadier Barnard of the Light Division asked him how much he owed for his dinner.

This policy, as the Prime Minister and Viscount Castlereagh knew, had proved as valuable as a dozen victories.

The French in Southwestern France found themselves quartering an Army of gentlemen.

The British Commander-in-Chief even invited the *Maires* of the towns where he stayed to dine with him—a thing never heard of in a French Revolutionary general.

The result had been fantastic.

Those who had fled came flocking back to their homes.

It was said that the British waged war only against men with arms in their hands.

What was more, the British paid for all their requirements.

Before long, the inhabitants were coining money, and fowls and turkey were selling for large sums.

The Commissariat, instead of being starved of supplies, was inundated with offers of cattle, grain, and fodder.

Almost as if the Viscount could read the Marquis's thoughts, he said:

"I learnt from the last despatch I received that the French Bankers have offered the British cash and credit."

The Prime Minister laughed.

"I can tell you something more; an English Officer who is there wrote:

" 'If this is what making war in an enemy country is like, I never wish to campaign in a friendly one again.' "

They all laughed, then the Prime Minister said:

"To be serious, Midhurst, if you were wise enough to give Wellington such brilliant advice in advance, I hope you can suggest how to save the men we are sending out to join Wellington from losing their lives before they have even fired a shot."

"How many ships have been attacked so far?" the Marquis asked.

"Four," Lord Castlereagh replied. "The first one was sunk and nearly all those aboard were drowned. The other three were prepared for an attack, and managed to drive off the enemy with, however, a number of casualties."

He sighed before he continued:

"As you can imagine, those in command at Portsmouth are extremely concerned about it. At the same time, it is hard to believe that information can be got across to France so quickly."

"The smugglers do not take long to cross the Channel," the Prime Minister suggested.

"And I suppose that nefarious trade is still flourishing!" the Marquis remarked sarcastically.

The Prime Minister made a helpless gesture with his hands.

"What can we do?" he asked. "Smugglers big and small operate at night on almost every inch of the South Coast. We have employed more Coast Guards, provided them with faster ships, and have a number of intelligent men trying to discover from which harbours the smugglers leave."

"And the result?" the Marquis asked.

"I think perhaps we catch one in twenty," the Prime Minister replied gloomily.

"And as, of course, you are well aware," the

Viscount added, "the goods they bring back to England are paid for in gold, which provides Napoleon with more arms and better guns with which to destroy our troops."

"I have also heard," the Marquis said quietly, "that the Smugglers bring back spies, and even assassins. So, for God's sake, strengthen the guard on His Royal Highness. His death would be a tremendous moral victory for Bonaparte."

Both men stared at him in astonishment.

"How have you heard that?" the Prime Minister asked.

"I have my ways of knowing things," the Marquis answered, "and I do beg of you to take care."

The Prime Minister sighed.

"There have been two attempts which, to put it briefly, were 'nipped in the bud.' But, of course, we are always vigilant."

"At this moment, when the tide is turning," the Marquis said, "your vigilance should be doubled. I can imagine nothing that would lower the morale of our men who have fought their way into France more than to learn of a disaster of that sort."

"I promise you, Midhurst, we are doing our best," the Prime Minister said, "but as we have already said, the Smugglers creep in, and we cannot always know what they carry besides the brandy and other contraband."

The Marquis thought he sounded rather feeble and ineffective.

The increase in smuggling was a disgraceful state of affairs, he thought, but he did not say so.

Instead, he said to the Prime Minister:

"You have certainly presented me with a very

tricky problem, but I will do my best to solve it. To be honest, however, I can think of no possible way that information about the movement of our ships, even if it is obtained from the men aboard them, can reach France even more quickly than the smugglers could carry it back."

"At the same time, the information does get there," the Viscount said, "and you have never yet been defeated in any undertaking."

"I hope that remains true," the Marquis replied, "but, as they say, there always has to be a first time."

"I pray to God it is not this one," the Prime Minister finished.

They talked for a little while longer about the good news from the battle-front, and then the Marquis left.

As he drove back the way he had come, he was thinking that never in his life had he been given a more difficult problem.

There must be a solution—of course there was.

But how was he to begin to find it? Where should he start?

The last question, of course, was answered easily—by leaving for his house in Hampshire immediately.

This was what he had to do, and he knew it was his duty.

He must therefore apologise to Lady Georgina for not dining with her to-night as he had promised.

When he reached Piccadilly he turned his horses up Berkeley Street and into Berkeley Square.

Lady Georgina and her husband had a very small house in Bruton Street.

It was so small that it was overshadowed by the larger houses beside it.

The Marquis calculated that the rent could not be a very high one.

At the same time, they had a good address, which implied being in Mayfair.

As he drew up outside the front-door, he took his gold watch from his waistcoat pocket and saw it was after twelve o'clock.

There was always the possibility that Lady Georgina would have gone out to Luncheon, in which case, he could only leave her a message.

He told his groom to get down and ring the bell.

The door was opened by an elderly servant.

The Marquis was informed that Her Ladyship had not yet come downstairs.

He handed the reins to his groom and walked into the house.

He had, of course, been there often, and the elderly servant, who had been tipped generously on various occasions, bowed obsequiously.

"It's nice to see Your Lordship, but 'Er Ladyship isn't expecting you."

"I am aware of that," the Marquis replied, "but ask Her Ladyship if she will see me at once, as it is a matter of extreme urgency."

He walked into the small Sitting-Room off the hall.

The old servant hurried up the stairs as fast as his arthritic legs would carry him.

The Marquis walked to the window and looked out at the small garden which lay at the back of the house.

It was used by quite a number of adjacent house owners.

He was, however, not seeing the green grass or the flower-beds filled with colour.

He was thinking of the British ships, carrying no lights, but being attacked in the darkness because the enemy had learnt of their whereabouts.

He was so deep in his thoughts that he started when he heard Lady Georgina's voice behind him exclaim:

"It is really you! I was not expecting such an early visit!"

"I know, but I had to see you," the Marquis replied.

She shut the door and walked towards him.

With the sunshine on her face, he thought how beautiful she was.

Her hair was dark, almost black, and yet it had strange lights in it which were picked out by the sunshine.

Her eyes were the dark blue of the Mediterranean.

She had told him laughingly this was due to her Irish blood which came from her Mother.

"They always say that their blue eyes were put in with dirty fingers."

Hers certainly were framed by long, dark eye-lashes through which she looked at him provocatively in a way which was irresistible.

As she reached him now, the Marquis's arms went out towards her.

She lifted her face.

He kissed her fiercely, feeling the fire on her lips as he touched them.

Her body seemed almost to melt into his.

Only when he raised his head did she say:

"What has happened? Why are you here?"

"I have to go to the country," the Marquis explained, "so it is impossible for us to dine together to-night."

"Oh, Dearest Michael, how can you think of deserting me when Walter is away, and we can be together the whole night?"

"I know," the Marquis sighed, "but unfortunately I have to go home. Something has happened which requires my personal attention immediately, and which cannot wait until to-morrow."

"Are you—quite sure of that?" Lady Georgina asked in a low, seductive voice.

Then her lips were on his, and her arms were round his neck.

He knew she was pleading in a way in which there was no need for words.

Only when they were both breathless did the Marquis, with a superhuman effort, put her to one side.

"You must forgive me, Georgina," he said in a deep voice, "but I have to leave you. It will not be for long."

"Let me come with you," Lady Georgina suggested.

Her eyes were looking up into his.

He could see the fire in them and knew only too well why she was talked of as being a Tigress.

She was coaxing him with every breath she drew, with every movement of her body against his, and with her lips that were inviting his kisses.

He looked at her for a moment before he said:

"I am sorry, my dear, but it is a question of duty."

"Duty—to whom?" she asked, and there was a sharp note in her voice.

"To myself," the Marquis replied.

He kissed her forehead lightly before he said:

"I meant to buy you, before we met for dinner tonight, a bracelet I saw in Bond Street, and which I knew you would like. You shall have it immediately after I return, and the ear-rings to go with it."

"Oh, Michael, you are so good to me!" Lady Georgina cried. "Even so, while I adore your presents, it is you I want."

"As I want you," the Marquis said, "but now I must go."

He put her to one side as he spoke and walked towards the door.

He had almost reached it before she came running after him.

Flinging her arms around him once again, and pulling his head down to hers, she said:

"I love you, and do not forget it while you are attending to anything so boring as your duty!"

"I will be back as quickly as I can," the Marquis promised.

Once again he set her on one side, and although she tried to prevent him, he opened the door.

"Take care of yourself," he said with a smile.

Then he was gone.

Only when she heard his footsteps moving across the hall and heard him speaking to a servant did Lady Georgina realise that she was defeated.

Angrily she stamped her foot.

How was it possible that anything called duty

could be more important than she was?

Then she remembered the bracelet and ear-rings the Marquis had promised her.

She told herself that if he was away for too long, he would have to produce as well the necklace that went with them.

She knew how lovely it would look around her long, white neck.

Going to the mirror over the mantelpiece, she looked in it, imagining how the jewels would enhance her beauty.

chapter three

THE Lord Lieutenant's house was an old one which had been added to over the centuries.

It was set in a large garden and approached through a Park in which there were a number of ancient oak-trees.

Odella knew it well.

The Earl was a friend of her Father's and she had often been taken to parties in the house with the Earl's grandchildren.

She thought now, as they drove up the drive, that as Lord Lieutenant he would be the best person to advise her.

He would know what she should do, and to whom she should report what she had discovered.

She did not, however, want to upset him, as he

had been in ill health and was growing very old.

But she could think of no-one else she could go to at that moment.

And every nerve in her body told her that time was important.

If she shirked responsibility or delayed in any way getting the information to the right place, many more men would die.

Thompson brought the carriage to a standstill outside the front-door.

Without waiting, Odella jumped out and ran up the stairs.

There was a little wait before the door opened.

The elderly Butler whom she had known since she was a child stood there.

"Why, it's Miss Odella!" he exclaimed in surprise.

"Yes, Hodgson, and I must speak to His Lordship!"

"The Master's got someone with him at th' moment," Hodgson explained.

"It is really very important, or I would not be bothering him," Odella replied.

"Then y'd better go into the Morning-Room, Miss Odella," the Butler said after a moment's hesitation, "an' I'll see what I can do."

"Thank you," Odella said with relief, "and I promise you I would not bother His Lordship if it were not something very urgent."

She did not wait for Hodgson to open the door, but let herself into the Morning-Room which overlooked the Park in front of the house.

It was a rather dull room, and she thought that when the Earl's eldest son inherited, he would have to do a lot of repairs to the house.

Because she was so agitated, she could not sit still.

She walked to the window to look out with unseeing eyes at the sun shining on the trees in the Park.

How was it possible, she wondered, that there were people in England who would betray the men who were fighting for freedom.

She thought how fervently her Father prayed that Wellington's Army might be victorious.

The news was better than it had been for some time.

That made it seemed incredible that men were going to their deaths, not fighting the enemy, but simply while sailing from one port to another.

"Something must be done about it!" Odella murmured.

The door opened, and she thought it was Hodgson returning to say that the Earl would see her.

To her surprise, it was the Earl himself.

He came into the room, leaning heavily on a stick. It was obvious that it was an effort for him to walk.

"Hodgson tells me you want to see me urgently, my child," he said as Odella ran towards him.

"I had to see you," she said, "and although I know you are busy, this is something desperately important!"

"Then let us sit down while you tell me all about it," the old man said kindly.

He seated himself in a high-backed chair in front of the fireplace.

Because she knew he was deaf, Odella went down on her knees beside his chair.

"I have just come from Portsmouth," she said, "and although it is . . . hard to believe . . . I discovered . . . a spy . . . there!"

"A pie?" the Earl asked with a puzzled expression on his face.

"A *spy*!" Odella repeated a little louder.

Although there was no need for it, she had lowered her voice.

It was because the information she had was so extraordinary that she felt she could speak about it only in hushed tones.

"A spy!" the Earl said, his eyes widening.

"Yes," Odella affirmed. "It is a woman and she is extracting information from seamen which enables the French Navy to be . . . lying in wait for . . . their ships as they leave port."

She spoke breathlessly.

Then she realised that once again the Earl was finding it difficult to hear what she said.

To her surprise, he got slowly to his feet.

"You say you have found a spy!" he said, determined to make sure of it himself. "Well, I have somebody with me to whom you must tell your story, as I cannot quite understand what you are saying."

He moved towards the door.

Odella rose and hurried to open it for him.

As he passed through it, he said:

"Come with me, my dear. The gentleman I want you to meet is in my Study. He is, in fact, the Marquis of Midhurst."

Odella obeyed him.

They walked very slowly through the hall and down the corridor which led, as she knew, to the Earl's Study.

It was with difficulty that she managed to walk as slowly as he did.

She felt she wanted to run simply because precious time was passing.

Nothing yet was being done to save the men whom *Madame* Zosina was ready to send to their deaths.

It seemed a long time before they reached the Study door.

Once again Odella opened it so that the Earl could go in first.

She was aware that a man was standing at the window.

As the Earl entered the room, it took him a few moments to realise where his guest was.

He first looked towards the chairs in front of the fireplace where he had left him.

Then, as the Marquis of Midhurst turned round, he said:

"My Rector's daughter has just called with a strange story which I think you ought to hear. I will therefore leave you together as I tell my Butler to bring you some wine."

He moved back into the corridor as he spoke, and Hodgson, who had followed them, shut the door.

Odella looked at the Marquis of Midhurst with interest.

She had, of course, heard of him and had read what the newspapers had reported about his two medals for gallantry.

As she walked towards him she thought there was something overwhelming about him which she had not found in any other man.

She could not explain it to herself, but she felt as if his vibrations made him seem taller than he was.

She thought that even in a crowded room one would have quickly been aware of him.

The Marquis, in fact, was rather annoyed at the way the Earl had left him.

It was just when he was trying to explain to him why he had called unexpectedly.

Aware of the Earl's deafness, he had been speaking louder than he usually did.

Then the Butler had come to the Earl's side to say that a Miss Odella wished to see him urgently.

He had been surprised when the Earl, instead of saying she must wait, got up and went slowly from the room.

Now, instead of listening to what he had come to say, the Earl had left the Rector's daughter alone with him.

As Odella reached him, he saw that she was very young and surprisingly lovely, but she was wasting his time.

He was well aware from what the Prime Minister and Viscount Castlereagh had said that it was not talk that was needed at the moment, but action.

The Marquis, therefore, said in a somewhat uncompromising voice:

"You must excuse me if I go and join my host, because I have very little time at my disposal."

"I can understand that," Odella said, "but what I was trying to tell the Earl is that I have discovered . . . a spy in . . . Portsmouth."

For a moment the Marquis thought she must be joking.

She had lowered her voice as she spoke, and the Marquis said with a slight twist of his lips:

"How did you know he was a spy? Was he draped in black and prying in a manner which made you suspicious?"

Odella stared at him.

Then, as she realised that he was making fun of her, she turned and walked towards the door.

She had almost reached it, when the Marquis said sharply:

"Where are you going?"

"To find somebody, My Lord," Odella replied, "who will listen to what I have to say and understand that I am trying to save the lives of the men who will be sailing from Portsmouth to join Wellington's Army now in France."

As she finished speaking, she reached out towards the handle of the door.

She was on the point of opening it, when the Marquis said:

"Stop!"

It was a command, and almost despite herself she turned back towards him.

"Are you serious in what you have just said?" he asked.

"I would not have come here to bother the Earl if I did not think that what I have discovered is not merely serious, but extremely urgent!" Odella retorted.

"Then I must apologise," the Marquis said. "Please come back and tell me about this."

Just for a moment Odella thought she could not be placated so easily.

Then she remembered that time was passing.

The ships leaving Portsmouth would be unaware that the enemy was waiting to attack them.

Slowly, therefore, she walked back towards the Marquis.

When she reached him she looked at him with an unmistakably hostile expression in her eyes.

"Suppose we sit down?" the Marquis said in a quiet voice. "Please forget what I said and tell me exactly why you are here."

Odella wanted to say that she preferred to stand.

Then, because he somehow seemed to force her to obey him, she sat in the nearest chair.

"I went to Portsmouth this morning," she began, "to do some shopping. When my maid and I were driving through the main street, we encountered a Circus Parade. They have set up their tents in Lincoln Field."

She found it hard to look at the Marquis as she spoke.

Her Mother had always told her she should look at the person to whom she was talking.

She was, nevertheless, aware that he was listening to everything she was saying.

She went on with the story, telling him how, when she had done her shopping, she and her maid had gone to where the Circus was performing.

She told him how they had decided first to consult *Madame* Zosina, the Fortune-Teller.

She described the arrangement of the chairs inside the tent, how the seamen were going in one by one to have their fortunes told, and finally how she had been able to listen to what was said when it was next her turn.

When she disclosed what she had overheard, the Marquis sat down in a chair beside her.

"You could hear quite easily?" he asked.

It was the first time he had spoken since she had begun her story.

"Not easily," Odella replied, "because *Madame* Zosina spoke in a very soft voice. But I was aware, because I, too, tell fortunes, how clever she was at extracting information from them without the seamen having the slightest idea what she was doing."

She paused before she went on:

"When the last seaman came out, a soldier asked if he could go in before me, as he had to be back in barracks by four o'clock."

She went on to explain what had been said to the soldier and what he had replied.

Ever since she had been small she had been taught by her Father to memorise poems and quotations accurately.

She had been made to learn the Collects every Sunday from the time she could read.

Her Father liked her to sing the well-known hymns in Church without referring to her Hymn-Book.

"The more you use your brain, the better it works" was one of the Rector's favourite sayings.

Odella thought as she repeated to the Marquis what she had overheard that it was exactly what had been said.

Only occasionally had there been a word she had missed.

She finished by explaining how the soldier, in the same way as the sailor, had been given a so-called talisman which would "keep him safe."

"What did you do then?" the Marquis asked.

"My maid, Emily, who had accompanied me, went in next," Odella said.

"And did *Madame* Zosina use the same technique on her?"

"No, she did not. She used the usual patter of all Fortune-Tellers, whether they are speaking the truth or not."

"Do you claim to be speaking as an authority, since it is something you do yourself?" the Marquis asked.

Odella gave a little laugh.

"I am hardly an authority, but I do tell fortunes at our village Bazaars, and people believe what I tell them. In ninety-nine cases out of a hundred my predictions come true."

"So you were aware that *Madame* Zosina was an expert at drawing out the secrets that simple men had sworn not to reveal to anyone."

"They had not the slightest idea that they were betraying their comrades or themselves," Odella said quickly. "They merely thought she was using some magic which is outside the rules and regulations given to humans."

"I suppose you know," the Marquis said quietly, "that what you have told me is vitally important and something has to be done about it immediately."

"That is precisely why I am here," Odella said. "My father is away and will not be back for about a week. The only other person I could turn to was therefore the Lord Lieutenant."

The Marquis got up and walked across the room.

Odella knew he was pondering what she had said.

She could not help thinking he was one of the most handsome men she had ever imagined.

She wondered, although she knew the Marquis's home was some distance away, whether her Father and Mother had known his parents.

He was obviously older than she was; in fact, she thought he must be twenty-eight or nine.

She would never have met him at children's parties, as she had met most of the other young men of any importance in the County.

The Marquis turned round once again and came towards her.

"I have been thinking over what you have told me," he said. "What we have to find out, and this is the key to the whole problem, is to whom *Madame* Zosina passes on the information she extracts from those who are sailing in the ships that leave the port."

"I realise that," Odella said, "and it must be that person who by some means alerts the French Navy."

The Marquis nodded, and she said:

"Please, My Lord, do something quickly! I cannot . . . bear to think of those men sailing to their . . . deaths before they have even had a chance of . . . firing a shot at . . . the enemy."

"I am trying to plan what we can do," the Marquis answered, "and I am hoping, Miss Odella—I do not know your other name—that you are brave enough and patriotic enough to do what I suggest."

Odella looked at him in surprise.

"W-what are you . . . asking *me* to . . . do?" she enquired.

"I am just working it out in my mind," the Marquis said, "but if I could arrange for *Madame* Zosina to be taken suddenly ill, would you take her place, tell the fortunes of those who consult her, and eventually meet whoever it is she contacts to pass on her traitorous information?"

Odella's eyes opened wide.

"T-take . . . *Madame* Zosina's place?" she murmured.

"You say you tell fortunes," the Marquis said, "and you described *Madame* Zosina as wearing a *yashmak* in the Circus Parade. It would be quite easy for you to take her place, as the public does not see her face properly."

Odella gave a little gasp, but she did not interrupt as the Marquis went on:

"I may be wrong, but I speak from long experience when I say that it is doubtful if *Madame* Zosina actually knows the name of the Agent to whom she passes her information, and she has probably never really seen him."

"H-how can that be . . . possible?" Odella asked.

"She is sure to be approached at night. I think it unlikely he would send a go-between, since he would trust nobody but himself with such vital information."

The Marquis made a gesture with his hands.

"I am only guessing, of course, but we have to play the situation by ear, and must always be ready to expect the unexpected."

"But . . . how . . . how . . . can I do what you . . . want?" Odella asked.

Even as she spoke she knew it was not impossible.

Her father was away.

If the Marquis could arrange to collect her from the Rectory, Mrs. Barnet would not be particularly surprised if she told her she was going to stay with a friend.

At the same time, it was terrifying.

How could she play a part which might be dangerous, or perhaps be considered ridiculous by any of her Father's friends if they discovered what she had done.

As if he knew exactly what she was thinking, the Marquis said quietly:

"You will be doing this for England. Would you ever sleep peacefully again if you knew you had let these two ships, if not many more, go to the bottom of the sea without trying to prevent it?"

"S-surely, there must be . . . somebody better . . . than . . . me?" Odella objected.

"Who?" the Marquis asked sharply. "You have been clever enough to discover what has been puzzling both the Prime Minister and Viscount Castlereagh."

His voice deepened as he continued:

"I am trusting you with my secret, Miss Odella, when I tell you that I have come here from London especially to find out how our ships are being shadowed as soon as they leave port and are attacked when they reach the open sea. By what seems a miracle, you have already brought me the answer, when I had expected it might take me weeks."

Odella's eyes were very wide in her small, pointed face as she said:

"It . . . does seem as if . . . God meant me to learn what *Madame* Zosina was . . . doing."

"I believed all the time we were fighting our way through Portugal and Spain that God was on our side," the Marquis said quietly. "On many occasions, when we found ourselves in an ambush that threatened to annihilate us, we escaped only by what seemed to be Divine protection."

Odella gave a deep sigh.

"Then I will . . . try to do what you . . . suggest, but please . . . please explain to me very . . . carefully exactly what will happen . . . because I am . . . very frightened."

"Of course you are," the Marquis said in a comforting manner, "but I will make it as easy as I can, and I promise you one thing—you will not be unguarded. There will be men within call ready and waiting in case anything should go wrong."

He spoke in a way that made it seem to Odella that he had already taken command and the whole plan was falling into place in his mind.

"What I am going to suggest now," he said, "is that you go home and say nothing to anyone—not one single word—of what is to happen."

Odella was listening.

She clenched her fingers together because she felt as if every nerve in her body was alert.

She knew she must keep her self-control and not interfere or argue.

"To-morrow morning," the Marquis was saying, "you will receive a letter asking you to stay the night, or perhaps two nights, with a friend whose name you will give me. Whoever is in your household will want to know where you are going. Is your Mother there?"

"N-no, my Mother is . . . d-dead," Odella replied, "and, as I told you, my Father is . . . away. There are only the servants. They have looked after me for many years and are naturally . . . interested in everything . . . I do."

"Very well," the Marquis said. "They of course must not be in the least suspicious that you are doing anything unusual. Give me the name of someone who lives on the far side of Portsmouth from your home, which is the direction in which they will see you travel."

Odella realised he was thinking of every detail, and she said:

"Mrs. Grayson is a friend of the family, and I did stay with her last year for a garden-party she was giving."

The Marquis walked to the desk, and taking a piece of writing-paper, wrote down the name.

"You will inform your household," he said, "that Mrs. Grayson has asked you to stay, and is sending a carriage for you at five o'clock. It will take you to the field where the Circus is taking place and you will go to *Madame* Zosina's tent, as you did to-day, and await your turn."

"I understand," Odella murmured.

"There you will find a man whom you will allow to go in first," the Marquis continued, "preferably when there is no-one else in the tent. Yet if there are other people waiting, it cannot be helped. Do you understand?"

"Y-yes . . ." Odella murmured.

"If you listen, as you did before, you will hear the man having his fortune told. Then he will invite

Madame Zosina to drink to the success of what she has predicted."

The Marquis paused before he said:

"When she drinks what he has offered her, he will leave her and you will take his place. A few seconds later she will collapse. Then you will call for a member of the Circus to be fetched."

Odella thought how embarrassing this would be.

At the same time, she said nothing.

"When the Owner, or someone in authority, arrives, you will tell him you were with *Madame* Zosina when it happened. You will say that you have had nursing experience, and you realise she has had a slight heart attack. You will suggest that she is carried to her caravan and you will go with her."

Odella was listening, her face very pale.

"Then you will say," the Marquis went on, "that she may be unconscious for several hours and you offer to take her place. You will explain that you have had considerable experience as an amateur Fortune-Teller. If the Circus people seem reluctant, you will say how much those who are waiting are looking forward to consulting *Madame* Zosina, and how disappointed they will be if she is not available."

"That is true," Odella agreed.

"You can point out that if you wear her costume and *yashmak*," the Marquis said, "no-one will doubt for a moment that it is not *Madame* herself telling them their fortunes."

He paused.

"It . . . it sounds feasible," Odella admitted,

"but . . . suppose I am . . . denounced as an . . . imposter?"

"Why should you be?" the Marquis asked sharply. "After all, when people go to have their fortunes told, they are thinking of themselves, not of the figure gazing into her crystal ball."

Odella knew this was true.

"A-and . . . after that?" she asked.

"You wait until the session is finished, then go to *Madame* Zosina's caravan, where she will still be lying unconscious. You may have to spend the night with her and I can only hope it will not be too uncomfortable."

He smiled at Odella before he went on:

"At the same time, I am sure she will be contacted by the Agent to whom she is passing on the secrets she has extracted from the seamen during the afternoon, and, supposedly, that evening."

"Supposing . . . he does not . . . come?" Odella said.

The Marquis did not reply, and after a moment she asked:

"Are you . . . s-saying I must stay on . . . still taking . . . *Madame* Zosina's place?"

"You will be given by the man who drugged her in the first place a small bottle containing another dose of what he gave her to drink. If you have not learnt what we want to know and she looks like coming round from her unconsciousness, you will have to give it to her."

Odella clenched her fingers until the blood seemed to leave them.

She wanted to scream at the Marquis that she

would not do it—it was too much to ask—far too frightening.

Yet she knew that if she did so, he would despise her utterly.

At the same time, she would for ever reproach herself as a traitor to her own country.

'There is . . . nothing else I . . . can do,' she thought helplessly.

Then, in a different tone, the Marquis said quietly:

"I know it is a great deal to ask of you. But if you had seen as many men die as I have, laughing and joking up until the last moment, and suffering incredible hardships, of which you, sleeping comfortably in your bed, have no knowledge, you would know, like me, that you would do anything—anything—to save the life of one single man."

"I have . . . said I will . . . do it," Odella murmured, "and I shall . . . pray that I . . . will not . . . fail you."

"I think you are very brave," the Marquis said, "and I feel sure that if anyone can pull this off, and I admit it is difficult, then it will be you!"

Odella gave a little sigh.

"I . . . I will go home," she said, "and I will . . . wait for the . . . the letter you are . . . sending me from . . . Mrs. Grayson."

The Marquis put out his hand, and said quietly:

"You are the bravest woman I have ever met, and if we pull this off, I will see to it that a large statue is erected to you in Portsmouth Harbour."

Odella laughed, as he had meant her to do, and it broke the tension.

Then she asked:

"What am I to . . . say to . . . the Earl?"

"Leave His Lordship to me," the Marquis replied. "I shall tell him that you gave me some information which may or may not be helpful, but which I will certainly bear in mind."

He smiled at her before he added:

"Incidentally, I no longer need his help now that I have yours."

"Now you are . . . frightening me . . . again," Odella said, "and please . . . please make . . . sure that . . . nothing goes wrong."

"You have to trust me," the Marquis answered, "as my men trusted me. And without boasting, I can truthfully say that I never failed them."

Odella walked towards the door and he opened it for her.

As they neared the hall, he said in a normal tone of voice for Hodgson's benefit:

"I know I have kept you talking for longer than I should have done, Miss Odella, and you want to get home. I will make your apologies to His Lordship, and I hope we can meet again some day. When the peace bells are ringing, I will give a large party at Midhurst Manor."

"I shall look forward to it," Odella answered.

She said good-bye to Hodgson and the Marquis escorted her to her carriage.

As Thompson drove off, she raised her hand in farewell.

No-one watching, she thought, would suspect for a moment that they had been hatching a plot which could only have come out of a novel or perhaps a melodrama performed on a stage.

"It cannot . . . be true! It just . . . cannot be . . . true!" Odella murmured to herself as she drove away.

chapter four

WHEN Odella was small, like most "only" children she had an imaginary companion who was always with her.

Hers was a small boy called Mickie, and as she grew older, Mickie grew with her.

He was still so much a part of her life that he gradually became in a way her Guardian Angel, especially after her Mother died.

She asked his advice and begged his help whenever she needed it.

Now, as she went to bed, she was talking to Mickie as she had when she was very small.

He became familiar to everyone in the household.

It was Mickie who was naughty and Odella who was good.

When she was six years old she tried to jump

the stream when it was swollen, fell in, and was soaked from head to foot.

Her Father was very angry with her, and said:

"It was extremely naughty of you to do anything so foolish."

"Mickie dared me to do it," Odella replied.

"If Mickie suggests anything so dangerous in the future, he will have to be punished," the Rector said severely.

Odella put her head on one side and asked:

"How will you punish Mickie, Papa?"

"I will forbid him to play with you for a week," the Rector answered, "and if he does not obey me, he will have to go away for ever."

"But I cannot lose Mickie . . . I cannot!" Odella had wailed.

"Then tell him to be good," the Rector said.

That night when he was alone with his wife he said:

"I am beginning to believe in Mickie myself. To Odella he is so real that she convinces me he actually is hovering in the background."

Mrs. Wayne laughed.

"I feel like that too. It is Mickie who does all the prankish things, and I think he has a great sense of humour."

Now, as she undressed and got ready for bed, Odella was talking to Mickie.

"Suppose I fail?" she said. "Yes, I know you will . . . help me, but it is . . . very dangerous, and yet it is . . . something I *have* to do."

She gave a little sob before she went on:

"How can I let those men be . . . drowned or shot by . . . the French because a wicked Fortune-

Teller has . . . extracted secret information . . . from them?"

As she pulled the sheets up to her chin she said:

"Why did I . . . go there? If we had gone to the 'Big Top' first, this would . . . never have . . . happened."

Almost as if Mickie were answering her, she knew she had been specially chosen to help and to save her countrymen!

The French were cruel and wicked.

They had over-run and forced into subjection countries which were not theirs.

Napoleon had, however, abandoned his plan of invading England with barges.

Odella had thought as a child ten years ago that God had deliberately made the Channel too rough for them to embark.

It must now have been God who had chosen her, because she could tell fortunes, to prevent the spy from doing any further damage.

The spy and *Madame Zostna* enabled the French to sink ship after ship before it could accomplish its mission.

"You must . . . help me . . . Mickie, you must!" Odella said as she tossed and turned.

In fact, she slept very little, but kept waking with a start, feeling she should already have left for Portsmouth.

* * *

When morning came, there was a letter which was found pushed under the front-door.

Odella read it and told Mrs. Barnet that she had

been asked by Mrs. Grayson to stay with her for one night, perhaps two.

"That'll make a nice change for you, Miss Odella!" Mrs. Barnet said. "It's good for you to get out. You be lonely when th' Master's away. Now, what are you going to wear?"

This was something that had not occurred to Odella.

She allowed Mrs. Barnet to pack one of her prettiest evening-gowns which her Mother had bought for her just before she died.

It was one she had never had the chance of wearing.

Mrs. Barnet chattered on, saying it was time she went to some parties and danced as she used to when she was a child.

"All the boys I danced with in those days," Odella replied, "are now grown up and are either in the Army or the Navy."

As she said the last word, she gave a little shiver.

Suppose she made a mess of what she had to do?

Suppose one of the men who would lose their lives was a boy she had played "Oranges and Lemons" with as a child?

She remembered how she used to enjoy "Musical Chairs" at the parties.

The boys thought it fun to push the girls onto the floor and stop them sitting down on a chair.

She was not interested in what Mrs. Barnet was packing for her.

She had, however, given thought to the gown she would wear to go to Portsmouth.

The Marquis had told her to say that she had had nursing experience.

She thought most of her gowns made her look young and rather frivolous.

She therefore chose a black gown she had worn when her Mother died.

It had a coat to wear over it.

"What d'you want to wear that for?" Mrs. Barnet asked in astonishment. "Surely Mrs. Grayson'll think it strange?"

"Papa does not believe in people mourning for a long period of time," Odella replied. "And Mama used to say our loved ones who had died were in Heaven, looking down on us and helping us."

She had gone on quickly:

"Mrs. Grayson might be shocked if I were not still in deep mourning, and there is no point in upsetting her."

"No, I suppose not," Mrs. Barnet said. "But I likes you in your muslins— ever so pretty you looks in 'em."

"Thank you." Odella smiled.

In the afternoon she put on the bonnet that went with the black gown which was trimmed with black ribbons.

It haloed her hair, which was the colour of sunshine, and made her skin seem dazzlingly white.

When Odella looked at herself in the mirror she had the idea that she did not look in the least like a working Nurse.

But she told herself consolingly that she did seem to have a little more authority.

At the last moment she remembered her Father's spectacles that he wore in the summer when it was very hot.

Because he worked so hard at his research for

the historical book he was writing, his eyes ached in the sunshine.

He therefore had a pair of plain spectacles tinted that seemed to take away the glare.

Odella put them on her nose in the Study and looked at herself in a gold-framed mirror.

It had been a wedding-present when the Rector and his wife were married.

Now, she told herself, she certainly looked very much older.

If she said she was experienced in nursing, nobody was likely to contradict her.

Then, as she heard footsteps approaching, she hastily put the spectacles in her hand-bag.

Mrs. Barnet opened the door.

"The carriage be at the door, Miss Odella," she said, "your trunk's been put inside and I've added a hat-box containing a pretty bonnet in case you changes your mind and wants to look more like yourself."

Odella gave a little laugh.

"I promise you I will take off my black if I find it is unnecessary."

She kissed Mrs. Barnet good-bye and waved to Emily, who was watching through the kitchen-window.

Then she stepped into the plain, rather ordinary-looking carriage that was waiting for her at the front-door.

She thought, however, that the coachman looked more important than the average coachman.

He did not speak to her, but merely touched his hat.

They drove off, Mrs. Barnet waving as they went down the drive.

Odella knew she was setting out on an adventure.

It was very frightening, because it was impossible to guess what would be the outcome.

Only after she had given a last wave to Mrs. Barnet did she realise there was an envelope on the small seat opposite her.

She picked it up and opened it.

Inside was a piece of paper on which was written:

> "HMS Heroic sails on Friday.
> HMS Victorious on Saturday."

She knew these were the names of the two ships she had to pass on to the spy.

She suspected they were non-existent, and that in fact no ships would be sailing on those particular days.

The envelope felt heavy and she found there was something in the bottom of it.

It was a very small bottle containing some ruby-coloured liquid.

She knew this was a further dose of what the Marquis's man would give to *Madame Zosina*, to make her unconscious.

She would have to repeat the dose if *Madame Zosina* came round before the Agent called to collect the information.

With a shudder of apprehension, Odella quickly put the envelope in her hand-bag.

Because she felt weak, she lay back against the padded seat.

She prayed first to God, then to Mickie for help.

As the horse pulling the carriage gathered speed, she thought she was travelling too fast to think clearly.

Yet she knew she had to have all her wits about her and be very, very careful not to make a mistake.

The Marquis had promised she would be guarded.

But it was difficult to guard somebody from a distance.

She was certain that if the Agent knew he was being deceived, she would be what was called "eliminated" in one way or another.

There had been so much talk of spies during the war that they had in some ways almost become a joke.

It was suspected that spies were brought to England by the Smugglers.

Sometimes, it was believed, they rowed themselves across the Channel.

Then they hid in creeks and at river-mouths, where they would be picked up by their friends.

As there had never been a spy in Nettleway, it was all just talk, no-one having been in personal contact with one.

However, her Father's research had taught him that this sort of thing had happened in the past.

Odella longed to discuss it with him now.

She wanted his advice.

At the same time, she knew that if he were aware of what she was doing, he would undoubtedly have forbidden it.

She had always been very carefully protected and looked after as a child.

Since she had grown older, she had not been allowed to go anywhere without somebody being with her.

She realised that Mrs. Barnet had been surprised that Mrs. Grayson had not sent a maid to accompany her.

In fact, after she had told Odella that the carriage had arrived, she had said as they walked down the passage to the hall:

"There's only th' coachman, but I 'spects you'll be all right with him. He looks a sensible sort of man."

"Of course I will be all right," Odella had replied. "After all, Mrs. Grayson does not live far away."

Mrs. Barnet made no reply.

But she had given a sniff which told Odella without words that she thought Mrs. Grayson was not behaving quite as she should.

As they neared Portsmouth, Odella wondered if the coachman knew exactly what was happening.

She wanted to ask if he had had any special instructions for her from the Marquis.

They were soon moving through traffic.

There were a number of people on the pavements as they drove towards Lincoln Field, which was not far from the harbour.

It was a large piece of wasteland which had never been cultivated and was used on all sorts of different occasions.

The Flower Show took place there.

There were Army parades which were too large for the Barrack square.

Occasionally there was a Mill that attracted too big an audience to be accommodated anywhere else in the town.

The last one, Odella remembered, was when Tom Scott, who was the champion of England, had fought the champion of Portsmouth, and not unexpectedly had been the winner.

They arrived at Lincoln Field.

It was then Odella realised that the Marquis had arranged for her arrival to coincide with the start of the performance in the "Big Top."

She could hear the music of the Band and also the noise of excited voices.

There were a lot of small boys hanging about outside.

They were trying to get a glimpse of the animals as they were led into the arena.

Some of them were lying flat on the ground in an attempt to peep under the wall of the tent.

There were several attendants shooing them away.

The rest of the field was quiet except for the chatter of some children who sat on the steps of the caravans.

They were parked some distance from the "Big Top," against a hedge.

The horses, the majority of them piebald, had been taken from the shafts.

They were cropping the grass, some tethered by the legs, others just wandering free.

The carriage did not stop, but drove on.

Odella realised it was taking her to the other end of the ground.

Here were a number of trees, but it was too far from the "Big Top" for there to be any caravans there belonging to the Circus itself.

The carriage drew up in the shade of a tree whose branches partially concealed it.

Odella did not move until the door opened.

Then the man said, speaking in a quiet, educated voice:

"I'll be stayin' here, Miss, all night."

Odella understood, and said in a small voice:

"Thank . . . you."

"If you go now into the Fortune-Teller's tent," the man went on, "you'll find a Naval Officer inside."

He then turned his attention to his horse, as if he had no wish for Odella to ask any questions.

She stepped out of the carriage.

A little way to her left there was a path which led from the road above the field.

She realised if anyone should see her, it would look as if she had come from the town.

She therefore walked across the field as quickly as possible, then took her time going towards the Fortune-Teller's tent.

As she had noticed yesterday, it was some way from the "Big Top."

She saw there was an attractive and colourful caravan parked by itself a little higher up the field.

She guessed this belonged to *Madame Zosina*.

It was where she would be carried when she was unconscious.

It was still early in the evening, and Odella expected there would not yet be many people in the Fortune-Teller's tent.

A man stood at the entrance from whom she had to purchase a ticket.

He was obviously a Romany with dark hair and dark eyes.

But he was getting on in years and despite his colourful shirt did not look at all attractive.

He took the money Odella offered him without saying anything.

He handed her a ticket, and drew aside the entrance flap of the tent for her to go inside.

There were only two people waiting.

The one nearest the glittering curtain that hid *Madame* Zosina was a young girl.

Next to her was, Odella knew, the man for whom she was looking.

He was dressed in naval uniform, that of an Officer rather than an ordinary seaman.

He was older than the young men who had been waiting ahead of Odella the previous day.

She sat down in the chair next to him, and as she expected, he ignored her.

He merely kept his eyes on the curtain behind which was the Fortune-Teller.

Three or four minutes passed before the curtain opened and a young man came out.

He was a village type, simple and obviously excited by what he had heard.

He put out his hand to the girl.

"Tis a'right, Kitty," he said, "we'll get our own way."

"Ye're sure o' that?" she asked.

" 'Er says so an' 'er knows!" he replied. "Come on, there be no point in wastin' any more time."

"Oi've not 'ad my fortune told!" Kitty objected.

"Yer fortune be m'fortune!" the man said. "Now, come on, Oi' ain't 'angin' around."

He pulled her somewhat roughly from the tent.

The Naval Officer then went behind the glittering curtain.

Odella moved up to the seat which Kitty had

vacated so that she could hear what was said.

In the same way that *Madame* Zosina had extracted information from the seamen and the soldier yesterday, she spoke in her seductive voice as she went into action.

"You have a great career ahead of you," she said. "One day you will be famous, and remember it was I who told you so."

"That's why I've come to see you," the officer said.

After a few more questions he told her there was just a chance—only a chance—that he would be promoted.

"You will be promoted, not once, but many times before you are finished with the Navy," *Madame* Zosina predicted. "Now, let me see—you are going to get the chance to show how brave you are in an emergency."

Then she began to draw him out to what he would be doing and where he was going.

It was done very cleverly.

Odella felt that anyone listening to *Madame* Zosina would be hypnotised into telling her anything she wished to know.

The Naval Officer allowed her to play her game to the full.

When she "guessed" the ship in which he would be sailing he asked in astonishment:

"How could you know that?"

"It is all here in my crystal ball," she replied. "And now to make you safe as you cross the Bay, I will send with you my magic powers."

She promised to be thinking of him and using her magic from the time he set sail from Portsmouth until he arrived at his destination.

"There will be a skirmish, or perhaps a battle when you land," *Madame* Zosina said, "but under your leadership your men will triumph and you will be rewarded."

Odella heard the Naval Officer give a sound of excited satisfaction, and thought how well he was acting.

"You've told me what I wanted to know," he said as *Madame* Zosina sat back, apparently exhausted. "Now I've brought with me a bottle of the best claret which my Father, who's a Wine Merchant, gave me. It's a claret that's been drunk by His Royal Highness the Prince Regent himself, and I want you to drink my health and to the future you've foretold for me."

"I will certainly do that," *Madame* Zosina agreed.

There was the sound of a cork being pulled from a bottle, then of wine being poured into a glass.

"Now, that's something worth drinking," the Officer said with satisfaction. "Please wish yourself the best while you drink it, as well as me."

The Fortune-Teller gave a little laugh.

"I will do as you say, and you must do the same."

"I'm ready to drink the bottle dry after what you've told me!" he replied.

He must have held out the bottle, for Odella heard a chink as if a glass touched it.

Then *Madame* Zosina said:

"To your Health and Happiness, Sailor, and may you get all you wish yourself."

"And all you wish me," the Naval Officer replied.

The Fortune-Teller must have drunk only half of what was in her glass, because he said:

"Now, 'Bottoms Up' for Good Luck, and if you leave that wine lying about, as sure as eggs is eggs, someone will sneak it!"

Madame Zosina laughed, then must have drunk what was left in her glass.

The Naval Officer scraped back his chair and said:

"I'll be thinking about you all the way to France."

"As I will be thinking of you," *Madame* Zosina replied.

He came through the curtain and to Odella's surprise did not even look at her.

He was carrying the bottle in his hand and sauntered along as if he were in no hurry to leave the tent.

As he passed the man who took the tickets, he said:

"That lady is a marvel—and that's the truth!"

The man did not reply, and Odella, rising to her feet, went through the curtain.

As she might have expected, *Madame* Zosina was sitting on what looked like a golden throne.

On either side were two huge candle-sticks.

They were like those Odella had seen in Catholic Churches, and the candles were lighted.

In front of the Fortune-Teller was a table.

On it was a crystal ball, similar to the one she had carried in the Circus Parade.

It was now set on a base to hold it in position.

Madame Zosina was still wearing her *yashmak*.

But it was difficult to see anything clearly in the flickering candlelight.

Besides the crystal ball there was a pack of playing-cards spread out on the table.

As Odella appeared, *Madame* Zosina asked:

"Do you want me to tell your fortune by the cards, or shall I look into my crystal ball and see what Fate has in store for you?"

"I would like the crystal ball, if you please," Odella replied.

She sat down on the seat in front of the Fortune-Teller.

"That is wise! The magic I see in my crystal comes from the stars."

Madame spoke in a dreamy voice, then bent over her crystal.

She suddenly put her hand up to her forehead.

Then slowly, very slowly, she toppled forward, knocking the crystal ball from its base as she did so.

For a moment Odella did not move.

Then when she realised that *Madame* Zosina was really unconscious, she opened the curtain and ran to where the man was selling the tickets.

He had just handed one to a young woman, and Odella said in a voice she hoped no-one else could hear:

"*Madame* Zosina has fainted! Get somebody to help me carry her to her caravan."

The man looked at her in astonishment.

Without saying any more, Odella deliberately ran back into the tent.

She looked back and saw that he was hurrying away.

With difficulty she raised *Madame* Zosina from where she had fallen forward on the table.

Then tentatively, because she did not like

touching her, Odella pulled the *yashmak* away from her face.

She was not expecting her to be young, but certainly not as ugly as she was.

Now she understood why she wore a *yashmak*.

Her face was thin and lined, and Odella guessed that when she removed the glittering crown and veils, her hair would be grey.

She waited.

It seemed to her a long time before the man who took the tickets returned with a woman.

They entered through the back of the tent behind *Madame* Zosina.

"Now, what's all this about?" the woman asked.

"*Madame* Zosina was just about to tell me my fortune," Odella explained, "when she collapsed. I am in fact a Nurse, and I have been thinking that perhaps she had a slight heart-attack."

"A heart-attack?" the woman shrieked. "Now, why should she have that, I'd like to know?"

"It can happen quite suddenly," Odella replied, "and as a Nurse, I can tell you that there is no need for it to be serious. In an hour or so she may be better."

"An hour or so?" the woman repeated. "That's a lot of use! There's already half-a-dozen people waiting to have their fortunes told."

"We ought to take her to her caravan and let her rest," Odella said. "When we are there, I have a suggestion to make which may help you."

"I doubt that," the woman said, "but it's no use her staying here. Luke, you'd better lift her up and get her away quickly, or everybody'll be asking questions we don't want to answer."

"Us don't want that, Mrs. Covey," Luke replied.

He picked up *Madame* Zosina quite easily in his arms.

She was not a big woman, Odella saw, and he carried her out of the back of the tent.

Mrs. Covey followed and looked back at the people waiting to buy tickets.

She was obviously wondering if they had noticed what was happening.

It was only a short distance to the caravan, and Mrs. Covey hurried to open the door.

Luke carried *Madame* Zosina inside and laid her on the bed.

It was a prettily furnished caravan, with a beautifully embroidered Spanish shawl thrown over the bed.

"Go back to the tent, Luke," Mrs. Covey ordered sharply. "Take the tickets, and if she's not better soon, you'll have to give them back their money."

"All right, Mrs. Covey," Luke agreed, "but Oi' don't know what Oi'm a going t' say t' them."

"Say nothing!" Mrs. Covey added in a sharp voice.

Odella was kneeling down beside the unconscious woman.

She took the crown from her head and released the veil that covered her hair.

It was dyed red, and it made her lined face look even more grotesque.

Luke had hurried away and Mrs. Covey asked:

"How bad is she?"

"I think she will be all right in a few hours, and definitely by to-morrow," Odella replied.

"To-morrow!" Mrs. Covey repeated, giving a

shriek. "And what am I to say to those as wants to consult her?"

"I was just going to suggest to you," Odella replied, "that perhaps I could be of help. I could take her place."

"You? What do you know about it?"

"I happen to be a Fortune-Teller," Odella replied. "Not a famous one, of course, like *Madame* Zosina, but I am well known in my village for making predictions which come true. I tell the future at Bazaars in the summer and Balls in the winter."

Mrs. Covey gave a gasp.

She must have once been a pretty woman, perhaps an Equestrian Ballerina.

Now she was getting on for fifty, and there were lines under her eyes.

"Do you really think you could take *Madame* Zosina's place?" she asked. "She's a good Fortune-Teller, and people come for miles to consult her."

"You do not want them to be disappointed, and I promise you, I can tell fortunes. They will have not the slightest idea, if I wear *Madame* Zosina's clothes, that it is not she who is predicting their future."

"It certainly seems as if it's Fate that you should be here," Mrs. Covey said, "and we're expecting a big crowd to-night. They'll make a fuss if they can't spend their money learning about th' future."

"It would be a pity to disappoint them," Odella replied, "and as I have nothing else planned for this evening, I shall be glad to give you a hand."

"We'll pay you, of course," Mrs. Covey said, "and we'll be grateful for your help."

"People will soon begin to ask what has happened," Odella said. "You will have to help me to dress."

She started to take off her bonnet as she spoke.

She was relieved when Mrs. Covey quickly divested the unconscious woman of her costume.

It was very like a cloak, and beneath it *Madame* wore only a bodice and a petticoat, not unlike what Odella herself was wearing.

She had thought she would keep on her black gown.

However, Mrs. Covey undid it at the back and obviously expected her to take it off.

It did not take long to put on the glittering gown that had looked so spectacular when *Madame* Zosina drove through the town.

Mrs. Covey covered Odella's hair with the shining veil and placed on top of it the crown with its crimson feathers and glittering gems.

She then looked at Odella with satisfaction.

"No-one'll guess in a million years you're not *Madame* Zosina herself," she said.

"Where is the *yashmak*?" Odella asked.

It was lying on the floor, and Mrs. Covey picked it up.

"So that's what you calls it," she said. "I only knows it as a 'nose-veil' meself."

She laughed and Odella laughed with her.

Then she said:

"In case *Madame* has not recovered by the time I have finished, I had better stay here with her to-night. It would be a mistake for anyone, even members of the Circus, to know that she is being impersonated."

"That's really kind of you," Mrs. Covey said. "And you're right, of course. If they talk, what they says will fly on the wind."

She made a gesture with her hands and went on:

"We'll have half of Portsmouth knowing that *Madame*'s bin taken bad, and that'll put the takings down—I can tell you!"

"Then let us keep quiet about it," Odella said, "and if I go back to the tent, even Luke will think that *Madame* Zosina has recovered."

"Oh, Luke's safe enough," Mrs. Covey answered. "I'll see he doesn't open his mouth."

She looked around the caravan.

"I'll bring you some blankets," she said, "and a pillow. You'll be comfortable enough on the floor, and as I've said, it be real good of you and something I won't forget in a hurry."

"I had better go to the tent," Odella said hastily. "I can see from here that there are more people going towards it, and the sooner I get to work, the better."

"You're a real sport," Mrs. Covey said, "and Zosina'll be ever so grateful. I promise you that."

Odella smiled at her.

"It will be a new experience to be dressed up like this. When it comes down to it, people always seem to ask the same questions about themselves."

"I bet they do," Mrs. Covey said, "and you tell them what they wants to hear."

She helped Odella, who was somewhat hampered by her flowing robes, down the steps to the ground.

Then they walked quickly to the back of the tent.

As she went inside, Odella could hear the people talking instead of sitting silently.

She guessed this was unusual.

Luke must have told them there would be an interval before *Madame* Zosina could see the next client.

Odella had only just settled herself on the golden throne when she heard him say:

"*Madame* Zosina's now ready t' receive th' gent'man in th' front row. Will everyone else remain quiet!"

There was an instant silence.

chapter five

ODELLA was beginning to feel very tired.

She thought she must have seen over twenty people.

Because she had concentrated so hard on them, she was finding it a strain.

She wondered what time it was.

It must have been getting late, because a number of her clients had said they must hurry to get home.

She felt distressed, knowing that one or two of the soldiers who had consulted her would not live for long.

But at least, she thought, they would die in battle, and not be drowned before they had even landed.

She could only pray, when she was not thinking

of the men's or girls' fortunes, that the Marquis was being active.

He must be making sure that the ships which might have been named by *Madame* Zosina previously were not leaving on the date and time specified.

But she could be sure of nothing except that eager faces one after another had looked up at her and said:

"Oh, tell me what's going to happen in the future."

At last she heard Luke's voice outside say:

"Come along now, Ladies and Gent'men, that'll be all for this evening. If you want to see *Madame* Zosina, you'll have to come back to-morrow."

Odella gave a sigh of relief and lay back in her chair.

Because she had so often bent forward pretending to gaze into the crystal ball, her back was aching a little.

She told herself it was important that she should see how *Madame* Zosina was.

She picked up her hand-bag which she had kept beside her on the golden throne.

She had not forgotten that it contained more of the drug which would keep the Fortune-Teller unconscious.

There was also in it the names of the ships she was to give to the Agent.

Odella was half-afraid that she had already forgotten them through concentrating on telling fortunes.

Luke did not come to speak to her, and she let herself out through the back of the tent.

In the darkness she could see only vaguely in the distance the last of the people moving away from the "Big Top."

They were laughing and chatting as they walked up the road.

She hurried to *Madame* Zosina's caravan and let herself in through the door, which was not locked.

There was only silence inside.

She found a candle-lantern which she had noticed before.

Having lit it, she could see that the Fortune-Teller was still lying on the bed where she had left her.

Her eyes were closed and she was as unconscious as she had been when Luke had first taken her there.

Slowly, because Odella was sure there was no need to hurry, she took off the shining garments she had worn and set them down tidily on a chair.

Then she put on her own black gown.

She wondered how long she would have to wait before the Agent came to collect what information *Madame* Zosina had been able to find out for him.

She knew that if *Madame* had been in her rightful place to-night, she would have been able to send more ships into danger, and with them the soldiers who were at that moment at Portsmouth, waiting to be carried overseas.

Because she had been thinking only about getting changed, Odella had not noticed there were some blankets in a corner that had not been there before.

There was also a pillow.

Investigating further, she found that on the table there was some food.

It was covered with a cloth, and when she looked

she saw there were sandwiches and a glass of milk.

She wondered if this was what *Madame* Zosina usually ate at night, or whether Mrs. Covey had ordered it specially for her.

She thought she should eat something, but she felt too nervous to be hungry.

The hour was approaching when she would see the Agent, and he would expect to be given the information she had discovered while she told fortunes.

Suddenly the horror of it seemed to sweep over her like a tidal wave.

She frightened herself more by fearing that perhaps *Madame* would wake up and denounce her, in which case, her life would certainly be in danger.

To make sure this did not happen, she opened her hand-bag.

She took out the envelope in which she knew there was the drug she had to give *Madame* Zosina if she appeared to be regaining consciousness.

She took out the little bottle.

As she did so, she became aware that there was something more in the envelope she had not noticed before.

She pulled it out.

It was, in fact, two or three lozenges, quite small ones, and she wondered why the Marquis had included them.

Then she saw that written on a piece of paper that enfolded them were the words:

"For a sore throat."

For a moment she stared at it, thinking it strange.

Then she understood.

The Marquis had certainly thought of everything.

He had realised, as she had not, that the Agent would recognise her voice as being different from *Madame* Zosina's.

Odella was certain the lozenges would not take away a sore throat, but give her one.

"He was very efficient," she told herself.

Then she shivered because everything that was happening was likely to lead her deeper than ever into the mire of deception.

She looked around at the things in the caravan and found a clock.

It was not a very expensive one, but it probably was more or less accurate and she saw it was after eleven.

She went to the window and saw that now all the lights on the "Big Top" had been extinguished.

There were only a few lighted windows in the distance belonging to the caravans.

This meant that the Agent might come at any moment, and Odella knew she must be ready for him.

She wished she had brought a cloak with her.

She knew it was going to be cold if she had to go outside.

All day there had been a little warmth of very early spring, but the nights were still very chilly.

It would have been sensible, she thought, if she had been wrapped up in one of her winter coats.

As she thought of it, she looked at the far end of the caravan.

In a dark corner, there was hanging what looked like a cloak.

She took it down and found it was exactly that,

a black cloak with a hood at the back of it.

She had the feeling it was what *Madame* Zosina put on to meet the man to whom she relayed her information.

Whether this was true or not, Odella decided it would be wise to wear it.

She could pull the hood over her forehead and hide part of her face as well as her golden hair.

The Marquis had said it was unlikely that she would be able to see the face of the Agent, but she could not be sure.

She could only pray she would meet him in the darkness so that while she could not see him, he could not see her.

She spread the blankets on the floor and propped the pillow against the wall.

Wearing the cloak with the hood over her head, she settled down to wait.

To make sure her face was hidden, she fastened the *yashmak* round her neck so that she could pull it over her nose at a moment's notice.

Then she had another idea.

She took the names of the ships from her hand-bag, read them several times to make certain she would not make a mistake, then blew out the candle-lantern.

She had to grope her way back to her blankets and pillow.

Once she was seated, she was aware there was just a faint glimmer of light from the stars shining through the windows.

There was not a sound from *Madame* Zosina, although Odella knew she was breathing, and was not, as she appeared to be, dead.

'Help me, Mickie, help me!' Odella said in her heart.

She was aware, although she tried to be calm, that the fear of what was going to happen was creeping over her.

It was moving through her breast and up to her lips.

She felt that if the Agent did come, she would be unable to speak to him.

'He must be here . . . soon,' she thought.

She picked up one of the lozenges and put it into her mouth.

It did not taste very nice, but because the Marquis had sent them, she forced herself to suck it.

When she had nearly finished it, she tried tentatively to say aloud:

"Hello."

There was no doubt her voice sounded hoarse and unnatural.

"I am ready and waiting," she told herself, "and the only thing missing is . . . the spy!"

If it had not been so frightening, she thought, she might have laughed at the idea.

She was a country girl who had never done anything adventurous in her life.

Disguised as another woman in a Romany caravan, she was waiting to talk to a French spy.

He was planning to destroy the ships that left from Portsmouth carrying men who were to join Wellington's Army.

Could anything be more fantastic?

And yet it was actually happening.

"I must be calm, very calm and . . . composed,"

Odella told herself. "Help me . . . Mickie . . . help . . . me!"

It was then there was a knock on the door.

It was loud, but a single knock.

For a moment Odella felt paralysed, as if she could not move.

Then she forced herself to put up her *yashmak* over her nose.

Slowly she rose and groped her way towards the door.

She opened it and thought for a moment that she must have been mistaken.

There was no-one there.

Then she saw the man who must have knocked was moving up the path that led to the road.

With difficulty, because there was no moon, she could make out the outline of a carriage.

Almost as if somebody were directing her, she knew what she had to do.

She walked down the steps of the caravan and onto the ground.

Shutting the door behind her, she moved towards the man.

He waited for her to appear, and when he saw her coming towards him, he went on ahead.

When she reached the road, she saw, as she had expected, there was a carriage drawn by two horses.

The man who had walked ahead was standing at the door.

As she reached him, he opened it.

There was only darkness inside.

Odella realised that there were blinds or curtains pulled over the windows.

She was obviously expected to enter, and as she did so she was aware of a strong smell of brandy mixed with another smell she could not for the moment identify.

Then a voice said:

"Sit down, *Madame*, on the little seat."

It was just beside her, and as she did so, the door was closed and now there was complete darkness.

Odella put out her hand to steady herself and found that on the seat beside her there was a large box.

As she touched it there was a rustling movement inside it, and she gave what was almost a little scream.

"It is all right," the man said. "It is only our little feathered friends, who have suffered somewhat from the roughness of our sea-crossing."

It was with almost a superhuman effort that Odella did not scream.

Now she knew—now she understood what had puzzled her and the Marquis.

Feathered friends! Why had they not thought of that?

Unexpectedly another voice spoke.

"If they can surmount the waves," he said, "so can I."

Odella had assumed there would be only one man to speak to her.

It came as a shock to realise there were two men sitting on the back seat.

This was the reason she had been told to sit on the smaller one.

"Was it very rough?" the first man, who she thought was the Agent, asked.

"C'était formidable!"

The answer came in French, and he then said in the same language:

"Elle ne comprend pas français?"

"Not a word!" the Agent said in the same language.

He bent towards Odella, and she could smell even more strongly the brandy he had been drinking.

"What have you to tell me, *Madame*?" he asked. "I apologise for being late, but as you have just heard, the sea was rough."

Odella reduced her voice almost to a whisper, and even to herself it sounded very hoarse.

"I have two ships for you," she said, "HMS *Heroic*, which sails on Friday, and HMS *Victorious*, which is leaving on Saturday."

"That is very good and, as you know, there will be two victories—splendid victories!"

"I will give you a third," the Frenchman said, speaking in his own language, "and one which is greater than any you have achieved."

"I hope you are right," the Agent replied, also speaking French, "but remember that Jacques and Henri tried and failed."

"But I am different," the Frenchman replied. "I have the *entrée*."

He spoke in a boastful tone.

Listening, Odella guessed he had been drinking more than the Agent had.

Now she knew that the other smell that was mixed with the brandy was the smell of salt water.

She thought when he crossed the channel his clothes must have got wet.

"I have here your reward," the Agent said in

English to Odella, "and of course there will be more when you have more information for me to-morrow night."

He was obviously feeling in his pocket for what he required.

He brought something out and put it on Odella's lap.

She held it and he said:

"Ten golden goblins for the first ship, and now ten for the second."

He started to feel in another pocket, but the Frenchman said:

"*Dépêchez-vous!* It is time we were on our way."

"The Post Chaise is waiting for you," the Agent replied, "and you will be in London easily by to-morrow afternoon."

"I must be sure of that," the Frenchman replied. "It is foolish to waste time."

The Agent found the other money and passed it to Odella.

As she took it, he bent forward to knock on the window, and the man outside opened the door.

As he did so, the Frenchman quickly slipped out and disappeared unobtrusively into the darkness.

He made his way, Odella supposed, to where the Post Chaise was waiting for him.

Then Odella managed with a little difficulty, because she was on the edge of the seat, to step down onto the ground.

She had no sooner done so than the man slammed the door to, climbed up onto the box, and picked up his reins.

The horses had been standing quite still.

Now, as he brought the whip down heavily on

their backs, they moved off at a great speed.

The wheels threw up dust and gravel.

It all happened so quickly that Odella was left standing on the side of the road, holding the money she had been given.

It was over! They had gone!

It was then she started to run towards the trees, where she believed the carriage would be waiting for her.

She was terrified by what she had heard, also afraid she would never be able to tell the Marquis about it.

The thought made her run faster than she had ever run before, despite the fact that she was encumbered by the long black cloak.

She pulled down the *yashmak* so that she could breathe more easily.

She pushed back the hood so that she could see better.

With a sense of relief she saw that the carriage was there.

The driver must have seen her coming, for he was waiting with the door open.

She was breathless as she reached him and he helped her inside.

As she half-collapsed in the seat, she realised somebody else was there and she gave a shriek of terror.

"It is all right," a quiet voice said. "It is only me."

It was the Marquis.

Because she was so relieved, Odella threw herself against him, saying incoherently:

"Oh . . . Mickie . . . Mickie . . . save . . . me! They

". . . will . . . kill me if . . . they find . . . out!"

The Marquis put his arms around her.

He could feel her trembling uncontrollably.

He lifted her legs up onto the seat beside him, holding her in his arms as if she were a child.

Because it was all over and she was safe, Odella burst into tears.

She cried tumultuously and helplessly.

The Marquis just held her close, feeling her body trembling against him.

"It is all over," he said. "You are safe and no-one shall hurt you."

It was impossible for Odella to speak.

Only as she felt the carriage moving and she knew that she was being carried away did she force herself to stop crying.

"I . . . I . . . am sorry . . . I am . . . s-sorry," she murmured, "b-but it has been . . . so frightening . . . and now I know . . . what has p-puzzled you . . . he is using . . . pigeons."

"Carrier pigeons!" the Marquis exclaimed. "My God, why did I not think of that?"

"They were . . . there in the . . . c-carriage . . . you must not let him . . . use them!"

"You are not to worry about it," the Marquis said. "The carriage is being followed."

His arms tightened for a moment around Odella as he said:

"How can I have been so stupid not to think of that myself? But it never occurred to me that they could be brought here in a Smugglers' boat."

It was then Odella thought of something else, and she cried:

"There was also a Frenchman with him who got out of the carriage before I did and slipped away into the darkness."

"A Frenchman?" the Marquis exclaimed in astonishment.

"Yes, and when . . . the Agent said that . . . the ships I had named for him would give him two victories . . . the Frenchman said he would . . . give him an even . . . greater victory!"

The Marquis stiffened.

"A greater victory?" he repeated. "Did he say what it was?"

"N-no, but when the Agent said that . . . Jacques and Henri had . . . failed he . . . replied that he would . . . succeed because he had . . . the *entrée*."

The Marquis was silent for a moment. Then he asked:

"Did he say anything else?"

"No . . . only that he was in a hurry . . . and the Agent assured him that . . . a Post Chaise was . . . waiting for him . . . and he would be in . . . London by to-morrow . . . afternoon."

There was silence for a moment.

"He was speaking in French. Was there anything you noticed about him in particular?"

"I could not . . . see either him or . . . the Agent," Odella replied. "They sat in the . . . darkness of the carriage with the windows . . . covered."

"But you listened?"

"Yes . . . and the Frenchman was . . . drinking a lot of . . . brandy. There was also the . . . smell of the sea . . . which at first I did not . . . recognise. It had been rough and his . . . clothes must have . . . got wet."

"And his voice?" the Marquis prompted. "What abut his voice?"

"It was deep . . . except when he . . . boasted. Then it rose . . . and . . . yes . . . his accent was definitely Parisian."

"And you yourself speak Parisian French?"

"Yes, my Mother was very . . . insistent that I should be taught the . . . very best Parisian French . . . although it . . . seemed somewhat . . . unpatriotic."

"Nevertheless," the Marquis said, "it has been of inestimable value, and a blessing for which we must be sincerely grateful."

Odella wiped her eyes with the back of her hand.

The Marquis took a handkerchief from his inside pocket and handed it to her.

"I . . . I am sorry I . . . c-cried," she said, "but . . ."

As she spoke she realised she was still in the Marquis's arms.

Her head was resting on his left shoulder, while her body lay across him.

Because it was dark and because it was comfortable, she had no wish for the moment to move.

All she could think about was that she was safe.

The Marquis was there, and no-one could hurt her.

She had managed to deduce from the way the Frenchman had spoken that he intended to kill somebody.

It had seemed as if the point of a dagger were piercing her heart, until the carriage had driven away and she was still alive.

"I do not want to frighten you," the Marquis

said, "but you know what we have to do now."

Odella gave a little cry.

"Oh . . . no! I cannot . . . do any more . . . I am . . . frightened, very frightened and . . . if they had . . . realised I could understand French . . . I know they . . . would have . . . killed me!"

"I promise I would protect you," the Marquis said, "and that is what I will continue to do. But you do understand, Odella, that only you can save His Royal Highness."

There was a sudden silence.

Then Odella said in a voice he could hardly hear:

"D-did   you . . . say . . . H-His . . . Royal . . . H-Highness?"

"That is whom I believe the Frenchman has come to kill," the Marquis said. "The two men who were mentioned had tried previously to assassinate him but were caught and executed."

"Y-you do not think . . . this Frenchman will . . . succeed?"

"Not if we denounce him."

"H-how can . . . we do . . . that?"

It was obvious she was very frightened again, for the Marquis could feel her trembling.

He held her closer.

"Now, listen, Odella," he said quietly, "all you have to do is to come with me now to London and attend a party the Prince Regent is giving to-morrow night at Carlton House."

He paused for a moment before he continued:

"It will not be as large as the parties he usually gives, but large enough for a Frenchman who has somehow managed to get himself invited to kill him when he is comparatively unguarded."

"You . . . you can . . . stop him . . . without me!" Odella cried.

"How can I do that when it is not I who heard his voice?" the Marquis enquired.

"But . . . I cannot . . . I cannot do . . . any m-more . . . I am frightened . . . very . . . very f-frightened!"

The words seemed to pour out of her lips, and she hid her face against the Marquis's shoulder.

"You have been so brave," he said softly. "So wonderful! I do not know of any other woman who would have behaved with such courage, or such *patriotism!"*

Odella drew in her breath.

There was a note of sincerity in the Marquis's voice which could not be mistaken.

She squeezed her eyes to try to prevent herself from crying.

Then she said in a whisper:

"I . . . I will do what . . . you want . . . but you will have to . . . help me."

"I will help you. I will be beside you, and I promise you no-one shall harm you."

There was silence, and Odella knew the horses were moving very quickly.

Like a child who is frightened of everything, she asked pathetically:

"Wh-where are we . . . g-going?"

"We are going to my house because, if you remember, your servants would think it strange that you did not stay the night with Mrs. Grayson, as they expected."

"And . . . when we get . . . there?" Odella enquired.

"We will leave for London. It will not be an easy journey, but I will make you as comfortable as possible. Then you must try to sleep."

Odella could think of nothing more to say.

She wanted to expostulate that she could not go to London alone with the Marquis.

She then thought it would sound foolish, when she had done so many things for him already.

It suddenly occurred to her how improper it was to be lying in the arms of a man she hardly knew.

And yet he seemed to fill her whole life.

She made a little movement.

As if he understood, he set her down beside him and pulled a fur-lined rug over her knees.

Then he took her hand and held it in both of his.

"We have to be very clever, you and I," he said, "and you must remember every word the Frenchman spoke—every intonation in his voice, so that you will recognise it instantly when you hear it again."

"I . . . I will try . . . I really will . . . try," Odella promised.

"There is something I want to ask you," the Marquis said in a rather different tone of voice.

"What is . . . it?" Odella enquired nervously.

"When you climbed into the carriage just now, you called me 'Mickie.' What made you do that?"

"He was . . . in my mind . . . because I had been talking to him all day about what I . . . had to do."

"And—who is he?" the Marquis asked.

Now there was a harsh note in his voice.

She was aware he suspected she had been discussing with somebody else what he had told her must be completely secret.

"He is . . . someone I . . . invented when I was a child," Odella explained, "but now I . . . think of . . . him as my . . . Guardian Angel."

"Your Guardian Angel!" the Marquis said slowly. "That is strange, because 'Mickie' was what my Mother always called me."

Odella's eyes opened wide.

"Your . . . Mother called you . . . Mickie?"

"My Christian name is Michael," the Marquis said.

"Oh . . . !"

Odella could not think of anything to say.

It seemed to her as if, in some extraordinary manner, Mickie, her playmate, her friend, and finally her Guardian Angel, had become one with the Marquis.

She could not put it into words.

Then, as she felt his fingers tighten on hers, she knew that was what had happened.

* * *

It did not take more than half an hour to reach Midhurst Manor.

By the time they reached it, Odella was sound asleep.

When the Marquis realised she could no longer stay awake, he had moved her again.

She now lay flat out on the seat with a cushion at her head and covered by the sable rug.

The Marquis seated himself on the smaller seat and was aware that she was completely and utterly exhausted.

He guessed she had not slept the night before,

and the drama of what had happened that evening had taken its toll.

The carriage drew up beside a long flight of stone steps which led up to the front-door.

The Marquis stepped out.

He ordered one of the footmen to waken the Housekeeper.

"Mrs. Briggs be already on the stairs, M'Lord," the young man replied, "in case ye required her."

The Marquis did not say anything.

He reached inside the carriage and gently lifted Odella up in his arms.

She was so light that he had no difficulty in carrying her up the steps, into the hall, and up the carved staircase to the first landing.

Mrs. Briggs was already there.

When she saw that the Marquis was carrying a young woman in his arms, she asked no questions.

She merely went ahead of him to open the door of one of the Guest-Rooms.

A footman who had followed the Marquis carried a lamp.

The Marquis laid Odella down on the bed.

"Let the young lady rest undisturbed while I have something to eat," he said.

"Shall I undress her, M'Lord?" Mrs. Briggs asked.

The Marquis shook his head.

"We are leaving for London as soon as fresh horses can be brought to the door. Arrange for blankets and pillows to be put in the front of the Travelling Chariot."

"Very good, M'Lord."

Mrs. Briggs hurried away.

The Marquis stood for a moment, looking down at Odella.

It was impossible, he thought, that any woman could look more lovely, childlike, and untouched by the wickedness and cruelty of the world.

And yet she had behaved with a bravery which he had never found in any other woman.

Then, because he knew he must not linger, he hurried from the room.

Going downstairs, he started to give his orders.

chapter six

ODELLA thought that her bed was moving round the room and wondered what was happening.

She opened her eyes and for a moment she thought she must still be dreaming.

She was lying down, and yet she could see the Marquis just where her feet ended.

It was then she realised that she was in a Travelling Chariot which was proceeding at a very fast pace.

She made a little sound, and the Marquis turned his head to look at her.

"Where . . . am I?" Odella asked.

"We are driving to London," he replied. "You have been snoring all the way, and I thought you would never wake up!"

"I do not snore!" Odella retorted indignantly,

then realised he was teasing her.

"You were like a quiet little mouse," he said, "and there is no reason for you to wake up. Just relax and go to sleep again and I will get you there safely."

It seemed incredible to Odella that she had not realised that he must have carried her from the carriage in which they had left Portsmouth into the Travelling Chariot.

She could remember that she had cried and that he had comforted her.

Now, unbelievably, they were on their way to London to try to save the life of the Prince Regent.

As if he knew she was going over in her mind what had happened, the Marquis said:

"You are not to worry yourself. I have everything planned and, if nothing else, you will enjoy seeing Carlton House."

"You mean . . . I will have to . . . go there?" Odella questioned.

"We are going to a party which His Royal Highness is giving," the Marquis said. "I had thought I would be so busy in Portsmouth that I would have to miss it. Now I can take you and you will find it is spectacular."

"B-but . . . how can I . . . ?" Odella began, thinking she had nothing to wear.

Then she remembered that Mrs. Barnet had put an evening-gown in her trunk that she was supposedly taking to Mrs. Grayson's house.

At the same time, it was fascinating to think she was to see Carlton House, of which she had heard so much.

She lay back against the pillows which she knew

the Marquis must have propped behind her.

As she did so, she was aware that she was not wearing the black cloak that belonged to *Madame* Zosina.

She was wearing a different one which was lined with fur and trimmed with ermine.

It certainly kept her warm, as did the fur rug which covered her legs.

Because she was small, there was just room even though the Marquis was driving for her to recline on the seat of the Travelling Chariot.

A groom was accommodated behind somewhat precariously.

She knew this because she had seen one of these Chariots when her Uncle had travelled in one to visit her Father.

If the groom was lucky, he also had a hood to pull over his head when it rained.

But she could not see him, and it was a strange feeling to be alone with the Marquis, and moving faster than she had ever moved before.

She was aware that the Chariot was drawn by four horses.

The Marquis was driving with an expertise which she knew would have impressed her Father.

He was wearing an overcoat with a high collar.

She could see his features silhouetted against the sky, and she thought again he was the most handsome man she had ever imagined.

He was just as she thought Mickie would look if she could see him.

"We are lucky," the Marquis remarked, "that the moon has come out and we can travel as fast as we could if it was daylight."

"Will it take us a long time to reach London?" Odella asked.

She was remembering that the Agent had said the Frenchman would get there in the afternoon.

"Not at the pace we are travelling," the Marquis replied. "Very shortly, we will change horses and you will have something to eat. I am sure you are hungry after all you have been through."

Odella remembered that she had not eaten the sandwiches or drunk the milk that had been left for *Madame* Zosina.

She had been too frightened to eat anything while she was waiting for the Agent to arrive.

Now she was feeling empty.

It would be nice to have just a little to eat, although she wondered what would be available in the middle of the night.

Now that the moon was out, everything was very beautiful.

The road looked like a silver streak winding away in front of them.

The Marquis's team was well trained.

Because he drove them so brilliantly, they moved in a manner which prevented the Chariot from bumping or swaying unnecessarily.

Lying back against the pillows, Odella thought this was part of an adventure that she would always remember.

Perhaps one day she would write it down in a book.

She tried not to think of what awaited them at the end of the journey.

She was afraid—really afraid—that she would not recognise the Frenchman's voice.

If he managed to kill the Prince Regent, it would be all her fault.

"Stop worrying!" the Marquis said quietly. "Enjoy this beautiful night, and know that there are no carrier-pigeons leaving Portsmouth to-day—or any other day!"

"You are . . . sure that your . . . men will have . . . caught the Agent?" Odella asked.

"I was assured they were the best men available," the Marquis replied, "and I cannot believe that your brilliance in discovering what was happening will go unrewarded."

Odella was silent for a moment.

Then she asked:

"And what . . . will happen to . . . *Madame Zosina*?"

"She will already have been collected from the caravan where we left her, and taken to prison."

Odella gave a little cry.

"She will . . . not be . . . executed?"

"You are not to worry about it," the Marquis said firmly. "Forget the Fortune-Teller and concentrate only on what lies ahead, which is, of course, that you must look beautiful and shine at Carlton House."

To his surprise, Odella laughed.

"Are you really expecting a girl from the country who has never been to a party in London to shine amongst all the sparkling, glamorous women who, I have been told, surround the Prince Regent?"

She sounded completely unaffected and unself-conscious.

The Marquis thought she was different in this way as she was in so many others.

What was more, she obviously had a sense of humour.

"I promise that you shall shine," he said. "And if you feel the gown you have with you is not smart enough for the occasion, we will beg, borrow, or steal one that is."

Again Odella laughed.

"I am not surprised you win all your battles," she said. "Confidence, my Father says, is something one always needs to be successful in life."

The Marquis agreed.

At the same time, he was aware that perhaps he was being over-optimistic.

Could it really be possible for this young girl to recognise the voice of a man she had heard only in the dark?

And what was more, a foreigner?

As she had been so frightened, it would have been difficult for her to think of anything but the danger she was in personally.

He thought as he drove on that Fate had certainly played into his hands.

He had gone to Portsmouth thinking the Prime Minister and Viscount Castlereagh had set him an impossible task.

There was only the faintest hope of his being successful.

They had all their people trying to discover why the ships that had left after dark should, the moment they were in the open sea, be attacked by the French Navy.

It had never struck any of them that the information was being conveyed to the French by carrier-pigeons.

Then, before he had even begun his investigation or explained to the Earl of Portsmouth exactly what he required, Odella had arrived.

She had given him the amazing information that she had discovered a spy.

'She is certainly a gift from the gods,' the Marquis thought.

Because he was so grateful to her, he was determined that she would enjoy herself at Carlton House.

He was quite certain that her beauty, which had astounded him, would not go unnoticed.

Then he told himself that it would be a mistake for her to be spoiled, or become self-conscious.

He glanced down at her.

He could see her very clearly in the moonlight that was shining into the carriage.

She was looking at him with wide eyes that seemed to reflect the stars.

"She is lovely, absolutely lovely!" he told himself.

Yet he thought it would be a great mistake if, like so many other women, she fell in love with him.

As the daughter of a country Parson, she could hardly play any part in his life in the future.

But he had no wish to leave her when she was no longer of any use, perhaps broken-hearted.

He was not being conceited. He was being honest with himself.

He knew how many women, like Lady Georgina, had fallen wildly in love with him as soon as he so much as looked in their direction.

But Lady Georgina, whom he had made his mistress, was one thing.

A pure, untouched young girl from a Rectory

was something very different.

The Marquis knew he must marry one day and have an heir.

But there was no hurry, and after the strenuous years of war, he wanted to be free to enjoy himself as a bachelor.

He had found so far that the women he met in London were like beautiful flowers.

They were only too eager for him to pluck them while they bloomed.

But they accepted it more or less resignedly when they faded and he turned to find a flower in another direction.

The Marquis had managed so far never to prolong a love-affair once it began to bore him.

The majority of women, like Lady Georgina, knew that if they lost him, there would be nothing they could do about it but accept it as inevitable.

Of course there were times, the Marquis admitted, when there had been tears and recriminations.

He had not listened to them.

He was sure, cynically, that there was always another man ready to take his place as soon as he left.

Yet now he was worried about Odella.

He knew perceptively that if she fell in love, it would be a very different emotion from that which he aroused in women like Lady Georgina.

To Odella it would be something sacred.

What else would she expect from a man whom she confused in her mind—or was it in her heart?—with her Guardian Angel?

"I must be very, very careful not to hurt her," the

Marquis told himself. "When she goes back to the Rectory she must just have happy memories of this adventure and of her time in London with which to beguile the man she will ultimately marry."

* * *

The Marquis drove his horses into the yard of a Coaching Inn.

Odella, who had not spoken for some time, asked:

"Are . . . we stopping . . . here?"

"I promised you something to eat," the Marquis replied.

"But surely . . . everyone will be . . . asleep at this . . . hour?"

He smiled as he drew his horses to a standstill, and then two ostlers came running from an adjacent stable.

"I sent a groom to ride across country," the Marquis explained, "which is quicker than going by road as we did, to warn them of our arrival. I will be very annoyed if my orders are not carried out!"

"You think of everything!" Odella exclaimed.

"For the moment I am thinking of you," he replied. "So hurry inside, and I expect you will find a maid waiting for you."

A maid was waiting.

She took Odella up to a bedroom, where the candles were already lit.

There was hot water in which to wash.

Now Odella could see the cloak she had been lent was even grander than she had thought it to be.

It was of royal-blue velvet, trimmed with ermine and lined with the softest and warmest fur.

As she took it off, she wished she had something more glamorous than her plain black gown to wear.

But she did not bother about herself for long, knowing that the Marquis would be in a hurry to continue their journey to London.

When she went down the stairs she was taken into a private room.

A large log fire was burning in the chimney and a table was laid in front of it.

The Marquis was looking exceedingly smart in his tight champagne-coloured pantalons.

His hessian boots were so highly polished that Odella was sure one could see one's face in them.

He smiled at her as she came into the room and, pulling up a chair, said:

"Sit down, Odella. I have ordered what I think you will enjoy, and then we must be on our way."

The hot soup was delicious, as was the well-cooked trout which followed it.

There was champagne to drink, which Odella had had before only on very special occasions, like Christmas and Birthdays.

Because she was really very hungry, she ate everything that was put in front of her.

It was delightful to be sitting in front of a warm fire.

When the servants who waited on them were not in the room, the Marquis said:

"I am interested, Odella, to know why your Mother was, as you said, so keen for you to speak French."

"She thought it was a mistake for English people to be so insular when they travelled—of course before the war—without taking the trouble to learn the language of the countries they visited."

"I think that is true," the Marquis agreed.

"So she had me taught French," Odella went on, "and also Spanish."

The Marquis was about to express his surprise, when Odella continued:

"Then, because Papa had no son, and he wanted me to help him with his research, he taught me Latin and Greek. I have always hoped that one day, if I am lucky, I will be able to go to Greece."

The Marquis was astonished.

Of all the women he knew, practically none of them had had a good education.

He had thought it impossible to discuss foreign countries or their literature, as he enjoyed doing, with anyone but a man.

There were a great many things, he thought, that he would have liked to talk about with Odella.

He was eager, however, to hurry on to London, and he was determined to get there in record time.

Wrapped in her warm cloak, Odella got into the Travelling Chariot, but now she sat beside the Marquis.

She had the fur rug over her legs.

The new team was fresh and set off at a tremendous pace.

It was impossible to talk intimately while they were moving so fast.

They made one more change of horses.

This time the Marquis reckoned on only a five-minute break before they were off again.

By now the moon was fading, the stars were disappearing, and the first ray of the sun was a streak of gold in the East.

It was so lovely that Odella felt as if she were travelling into a magical land.

There were no problems ahead, but only happiness.

Without being aware of it, she moved a little nearer to the Marquis.

Looking down at her, he said:

"You are all right? You are not too tired?"

"I am . . . thinking how . . . enchanted everything . . . looks," Odella replied.

There was a rapt note in her voice which the Marquis did not miss.

"That is what we will try to make it," he said. "We are setting out on a crusade together to destroy what is evil and to protect what is good."

"That is . . . what I want . . . to do," Odella murmured.

She looked up at him as she spoke.

He knew by the expression in her eyes that she was seeing him as a Knight in Shining Armour going into battle.

'I must protect her from being hurt or disillusioned,' he thought. "Not only by what we have to do but also by—me."

*　　*　　*

It was eight o'clock in the morning and the sun was now shining in a clear sky.

The Marquis turned his horses into Berkeley Square and stopped outside one of the more important-looking houses.

As he did so, a red carpet was rolled across the pavement.

Odella could see waiting there a number of

servants in smart livery, as well as an elderly Butler.

The Marquis helped Odella out of the chariot, and they walked through the front-door together.

"Good-morning, M'Lord!" the Butler said respectfully. "Your Lordship's orders arrived about an hour ago."

The Marquis nodded and took Odella up the staircase. Waiting at the top was the Housekeeper, wearing rustling black silk, with the silver chatelaine at her waist.

She curtsied to the Marquis, and he said:

"Good-morning, Mrs. Peel. You have prepared a room for Miss Wayne?"

"I have indeed, M'Lord."

The Housekeeper hurried ahead to open the door of a room along the passage.

As they walked after her, the Marquis said quietly:

"I want you to go to bed and sleep until the afternoon. Remember, we will be late tonight, and I want you to look your best."

Odella nodded, and he went on:

"We will have tea together in the *Boudoir*. Then I will tell you exactly what I have found out."

He lowered his voice as he spoke the last words.

When they reached the door of the room where Mrs. Peel was waiting, he walked on down the passage.

With difficulty, Odella stifled a desire to hang on to him and ask him to stay with her.

But she was already inside the room, and Mrs. Peel had shut the door.

"Let me help you undress, Miss," she said. "The

footman will be bringing up your trunk, and, on His Lordship's instructions, your breakfast."

It was much easier, Odella decided, to carry out His Lordship's orders than to think for herself.

She ate the breakfast which had been provided for her, then got into bed.

Mrs. Peel pulled down the blinds over the windows and drew the curtain to darken the room.

Odella had expected to lie awake thinking of all that had happened, but she fell asleep almost at once.

*　　*　　*

The Marquis went to his own room, where his valet was waiting for him.

He also ate a breakfast before he undressed and got into bed.

"I will sleep for four hours, Watkins," he said. "Tell them to have a light Luncheon prepared for me then, and my Phaeton round at two o'clock."

"Very good, M'Lord,"

Watkins had been the Marquis's Batman when he was in Wellington's Army.

He knew by the Marquis's voice and the expression on his face that "something was up."

He was intensely curious, but he was too well trained to ask questions.

He knew only that his Master was "on the war-path."

He was quite confident, whatever the difficulties that lay ahead, His Lordship would win through.

The Marquis had trained himself during the war to relax completely whenever he had the chance.

As it was usually a case of having no more than two or three hours sleep at a time, it was important that he should not waste the opportunity.

He therefore slept deeply until Watkins called him.

He awoke, aware that what lay ahead in the next few hours was vitally important.

He would need all his wits to cope with it.

He appeared, however, completely at his ease when dressed extremely smartly with a high cravat tied in a new and intricate manner he walked down the stairs.

His Phaeton was waiting at the door.

He could not resist admiring once again his two new horses that were drawing it.

As he stepped into the driving-seat, he said to the Butler:

"I hope to be back by four o'clock to have tea with my guest in the *Boudoir*."

"Very good, M'Lord," the Butler replied.

He bowed as the Marquis drove off, thinking, as he had often thought before, that there was no-one in London who could compare with the smartness of his Master.

The Marquis drove to Carlton House.

As he entered the courtyard he saw that preparations for the evening festivities were already under way.

The door was opened by one of the Prince Regent's servants wearing his dark-blue livery.

The Marquis, however, asked not for His Royal Highness, but for his Secretary, Colonel John McMahon.

"The Colonel's in his room, M'Lord," the serv

who had seen the Marquis before replied, "and his Assistant is with him."

"Take me to them," the Marquis ordered.

He knew that Colonel McMahon's assistant was General Sir Tomkins Turner, who had been in the same Regiment as himself.

He thought he, at least, would be extremely helpful.

Both the gentlemen were surprised when the Marquis was announced.

Colonel McMahon rose to his feet, saying:

"I am delighted to see you, My Lord! His Royal Highness asked for you yesterday, but was told you had gone to the country. We were half-afraid that you would not be with us this evening."

"I am certainly coming to the party," the Marquis replied, "but first I have news of grave importance to impart to you both."

He shook hands with the General as he spoke and said:

"What I have to tell you must be in the strictest confidence."

The eyes of the two men listening to him widened.

However, they understood.

Colonel McMahon went to the door of the adjoining room and told his Secretary to see that they were not disturbed.

He was also to make sure there was no-one lingering in the corridor outside.

He had known before that because the servants were curious as to what was taking place, they sometimes listened at key-holes.

It was not for any discreditable motive, but

simply because they wanted to be the first to know what His Royal Highness was likely to do next.

Also, of course, if there was any particularly arduous work for them to do which they had not anticipated.

When the Colonel sat down again, he said to the Marquis:

"Now you can speak without fear of being overheard."

The Marquis told them briefly and in a low voice what had occurred in Portsmouth.

When they learned about the carrier-pigeons, the General exclaimed:

"Why did no-one think of that?"

"That is what I have been asking myself," the Marquis replied, "but there is more to the story."

He then related what Odella had heard the Frenchman say to the Agent.

He was aware that both men stiffened as they listened.

"Another attempt!" Colonel McMahon groaned. "How can Bonaparte be so insistent that that is what he wants?"

"He is desperate," the Marquis answered. "Unless something unforeseen happens, it is only a question of months before the war ends. The death of the Prince Regent would certainly delay, or perhaps turn in another direction, the tide which is flowing in our favour."

"That is true," the General agreed. "What do you want us to do about this assassin?"

"First," the Marquis answered, "I want to see a list of everyone who has been invited here to-night."

Colonel McMahon rose, and taking a file of papers

from a filing-cabinet behind him, set it down in front of the Marquis.

The names were clearly written down in alphabetical order.

The Marquis went through them, looking for a foreign name.

The Prince Regent had always been particularly kind to the *émigrés* who had come to England during the Revolution.

Because they disliked the man they called "that upstart Corsican Corporal" who was ruling France, they had not returned during the Armistice.

At the party the Prince Regent had given in June, 1811, to celebrate the inauguration of his Regency, the *émigrés* had been given very special attention and places of honour.

The Marquis had been in Portugal at the time, but he remembered receiving a letter from his Father, telling him about the Grande Fête at Carlton House.

At the time he had been in a precarious position, with his troops on a rugged ledge of the Mountains.

Also, and it was quite usual, there was an acute shortage of food.

The lavishness of the entertainment at Carlton House in London had amused him.

The English from the top downwards had no idea of how the soldiers were suffering in their efforts to beat a tyrant who was determined to conquer Britain.

The 3rd Marquis of Midhurst had written to his son:

"The Prince of Wales announced on the 19th June that the Fête he had planned to take place at Carlton

*House would be ostensibly in honour of the exiled
Royal Family of France. "*

Reading the letter, his son thought this was
typical of the Prince, and he read on:

*"Two thousand invitations were hastily des-
patched—some to people who are no longer living!
When your Mother and I arrived, it was to find the
Bands of the Guards playing in the courtyard, and
Pall Mall, St. James's Street, and the Haymarket were
blocked with carriages."*

He had gone on to describe how the Regent had
received his guests in a room hung with blue silk
and decorated with gold fleur-de-lis.

*"All the émigrés were there, the Ducs de Berri, de
Bourbon, and d'Angoulême, the Prince de Condé, the
Comtes de Lisle and d'Artois, besides Louis XVI's
only surviving child, the Duchesse d'Angoulême."*

The Marquis had thought when he read the letter
that the Prince Regent had certainly done the French
of the *ancien régime* proud.

He thought it was a pity that the French
under Napoleon's orders did not appreciate the
compliment.

He looked down now at the list of names.

Starting with A, he found that now, three years
later, the *Comte* d'Artois had been invited, and the
Duc d'Angoulême.

Under the B's there was the *Duc* de Bourbon, and
under the C's the Prince de Condé.

He continued on down the list.

Then he came upon the *Comte* Jean de Lisle.

He studied the name for a moment before he remarked:

"I may be wrong, but I thought the *Comte* de Lisle was dead. I remember my Father saying he was an old man when he talked to him at supper during the Grande Fête of 1811."

"Yes, *he* is dead," the General replied, "but I gather this is a relative."

"Have you met him?" the Marquis enquired.

The General shook his head.

"No, I do not think he has been to Carlton House before, but I believe he is staying as a guest of Walter Langford, and his wife, Lady Georgina, who, you know, is the daughter of the Duke of Cumbria."

The Marquis was silent.

He was thinking.

He suddenly remembered that when he had first visited Lady Georgina at her house in Bruton Street, she had said:

"Our house is very small, but quite big enough. If one has a large house in Mayfair, one invariably has to have people to stay, not because they wish to see one, but because they want to be in London."

The Marquis knew this was true, for he was continually being asked to put up a relative for a a few days.

When they arrived, if they were at all popular, he hardly ever saw them.

"I am therefore able to say no to all requests for a free bed," Lady Georgina went on, "except, of course, to some of Walter's friends."

She laughed before she added:

"If he invites someone, he has to give up his Dressing-Room—but he makes them 'pay through the nose' for it!"

The Marquis could understand that Walter Langford, who was always short of cash, would not give up his Dressing-Room unless he was paid.

Now it struck him as strange that the *Comte* Jean de Lisle would pay to stay with Walter Langford rather than with his own relatives.

As he had seen, there were a number of other French friends and relatives coming to the party.

Yet perhaps he could not be accommodated by any of them.

He told himself he was being unduly suspicious, and continued down the list.

He found two other French names, *Monsieur* de Queyrac and the *Comte* de Valena, on whom he knew they must keep a strict eye.

He had finished and put the list to one side, when the General said:

"Do you intend to speak to His Royal Highness about this?"

"Of course," the Marquis replied. "You know as well as I do that nothing annoys him more than if plans are made behind his back, and he is not 'in the know,' so to speak."

The two men listening knew this was true.

"Very well, come along," the General said. "I will take you to him. But for Heaven's sake, make quite certain that he attends to what you have to say. Our job is difficult enough as it is, but at times His Royal Highness seems deliberately to court danger."

The Marquis smiled.

The reason was that the Prince Regent disliked being over-protected.

He had been warned several times that the French wished to assassinate him.

He had merely remarked that they would be lucky if they could evade the restrictions he had to put up with at Carlton House.

"Try your best to make him understand that he really must be careful," the General begged as he led the Marquis along the corridor.

"I will talk to him like a 'Dutch Uncle,' " the Marquis promised.

However, instead of being amused by this remark, the General looked no less worried.

chapter seven

ODELLA awoke as Mrs. Peel was pulling back the curtains.

She lay feeling as if she had slept for a very long time.

Two housemaids carried in a bath which they set down in front of the fireplace.

Mrs. Peel had insisted that they light the fire.

"It's been sunny to-day," she said, "but there's a definite nip in the air."

To Odella it was a delightful luxury to have her bath in front of the fire.

It had been scented with Oil of Violets, which Mrs. Peel told her came from the Marquis's house in Hampshire.

After her bath she put on one of the simple but pretty muslin gowns which had been packed for her to take to Mrs. Grayson's.

Feeling excited, she went into the *Boudoir*.

The table was already laid in front of the sofa with what she saw was a large and delicious tea.

The only items missing at the moment were the silver teapot and the kettle which she knew would be brought in when the Marquis arrived.

She thought the *Boudoir* was very attractive, and it was decorated with vases of hot-house flowers which scented the air.

As she looked round she saw that lying on a stool in front of the fireplace were the newspapers.

The sight of *The Times* and *The Morning Post* made her feel guilty.

When her Father was at home he was insistent that she should read the news every day.

"We may live in a small village, in what people think of as 'the back of beyond,' " he said, "but we can keep abreast of the situation both here and on the Continent if we read the newspapers."

On his insistence, Odella read not only the news, but also the Editorials every day.

She was aware now that since her Father had left and she had been so involved with the Marquis, she had not looked at a paper.

Hastily, she picked up *The Morning Post* and read the headlines.

Then, because she was curious about to-night's reception at Carlton House, she turned to the page that was headed *Court Circular*.

She thought perhaps there would be a list of the distinguished people she would see when she got there.

She had, however, only just started to read what

was printed on that page when the door opened and the Marquis came in.

She could not help giving a little cry of excitement.

He shut the door behind him and came towards her.

"I am back," he said, "and I have a great deal to tell you."

"Is . . . is it good news . . . or bad?" Odella asked.

Before the Marquis could reply, the Butler came in carrying a silver teapot followed by a footman with a kettle.

They placed these down on the large silver tray.

Already on it was the tea in a silver box, and jugs containing cream and milk besides a sugar bowl.

Odella could not help thinking it was all very elaborate for two people, but she knew it was what the Marquis expected.

"Now you pour out," he said, "and I am sure, unless you have had some Luncheon, you are hungry."

"I had a very large breakfast," Odella replied, "then I slept until less than an hour ago."

"That is exactly what I wanted you to do," the Marquis said. "We are going to have to be very clever this evening, so we will need all our wits about us."

The way he spoke made Odella look at him nervously.

Then, before he could say any more, the door was flung open and a Vision came into the room.

Staring in surprise, Odella thought she had never seen anyone look so beautiful and, at the same time, so flamboyant.

"Michael!" the Vision exclaimed. "I saw your Phaeton driving away from your front-door and knew you had returned."

Lady Georgina seemed to glide across the room towards the Marquis with both hands outstretched.

She was wearing a gown of vivid green satin and her bonnet was decorated with green ostrich feathers which fluttered as she moved.

There were huge emeralds glittering in her ears.

She wore an emerald necklace which flashed with green fire, as did the bracelet that decorated her left wrist.

While the Marquis rose slowly to his feet, Odella could only gasp because she had never seen anyone looking so fantastic.

"I have only just returned to London," the Marquis said.

"And I know you were coming to see me," Lady Georgina said in a soft, caressing voice.

The Marquis perfunctorily raised one of her hands to his lips.

Then he said:

"I am, as it happens, very busy, Georgina."

"But not too busy to see me!" Lady Georgina protested. "How could you be?"

She looked up at him, her head thrown back, her red lips parting provocatively.

The Marquis was suddenly aware that Odella was watching them wide-eyed.

As she glanced in her direction, Lady Georgina said in a very different tone of voice:

"Who is this? And why is she here?"

There was a sharpness in her tone which was unmistakable.

Odella drew in her breath.

"Allow me to introduce to you Miss Odella Wayne, who is one of my relatives," the Marquis said quietly. "She is coming with me to the party at Carlton House this evening, and will be staying here to-night."

"And I suppose she is chaperoned!" Lady Georgina said with again that sharp note in her voice.

"Naturally!" the Marquis answered. "You must understand that as I have a great deal to say to my relatives, who have only just arrived, I must now escort you to your carriage."

It seemed for a moment as if Lady Georgina were going to refuse to leave.

Then, tossing her head and ignoring Odella, she walked towards the door while the Marquis followed.

Outside in the corridor she said in a whisper:

"I must see you, Michael. You know how much I have missed you."

"We will talk about that later," the Marquis replied.

Lady Georgina, however, stopped.

"Walter is going away to-morrow."

"Again?" the Marquis exclaimed. "Where is he going?"

"To the South Coast on some business or other," Lady Georgina said, "so we can be together."

The Marquis did not answer.

He moved towards the stairs, and Lady Georgina was obliged to follow him.

As the Butler and two footmen were in the hall, they went down in silence.

Only when they had passed through the front-door did Lady Georgina stop at the top of the steps.

In a voice that only the Marquis could hear she said:

"To-morrow night—seven-thirty—and I shall be counting the hours, dearest wonderful Michael, until then."

The Marquis helped her into her carriage.

She waved to him as she drove off, but he made no response.

He was frowning as he walked back into the house.

He knew as he went back upstairs that Lady Georgina had been a shock to Odella.

He was sure that in the quiet life she had lived in the country she had never seen anyone like her.

Lady Georgina both looked different, and also behaved in a manner that was, to say the least of it, indiscreet.

The Marquis was right in thinking that Odella had been shocked.

More than that!

When the Marquis followed Lady Georgina from the room, Odella had thought despairingly that this was obviously the woman he loved.

She had, of course, heard when she was in the country of the smart, sophisticated Ladies of London Society.

But she had never seen one before.

Lady Georgina had therefore been a revelation.

As the door closed behind her and the Marquis, Odella had jumped up from the table and run into her bedroom.

She did not understand her feelings; she knew only that she felt upset and distressed.

She was acutely aware of the way Lady Georgina had spoken to the Marquis in that soft, caressing voice.

And of the way she had looked at him.

"She loves . . . him!" Odella told herself.

Then she realised that of course he must love her too.

How could he help being fascinated by anyone who was so beautiful, so elegant?

It seemed to Odella that Lady Georgina's eyes had glittered like her emeralds.

"Of . . . course he . . . loves her!" she told herself again. "H-how . . . could he do . . anything else, when she is so . . . very . . . very . . . beautiful?"

There was a sudden strange pain in her breast.

Because it startled her and was frightening, she said:

"Help me . . . help me . . . Mickie. What do . . . I do about it?"

Suddenly she was aware that Mickie was not there; he had somehow become the Marquis.

It was then she knew that if she had lost the Marquis, she had lost Mickie too.

* * *

When the Marquis returned to the *Boudoir*, he found it empty.

He wondered if he should ask Odella to return to him.

Then he decided that it might make things more awkward than they were already.

* * *

Odella was not aware that the Marquis had returned to the *Boudoir*.

She had stayed in her bedroom.

She felt as if she had received an unexpected blow on the head and did not know what to do about it.

"How can I be so foolish as to be hurt and upset," she asked herself, "because the Marquis loves somebody who belongs to his own world, which is so different from mine?"

However, she knew now, if she was honest, that she loved the Marquis.

Then she told herself despairingly that she might just as well love the Man in the Moon.

'When this is over, he will send me back to the country, and I will never see him again,' she thought. 'Anyway, why should he be interested in me?'

It was something she went on asking herself as Mrs. Peel helped her to dress.

Fortunately the gown which had been packed for the evening with Mrs. Grayson was very attractive.

Odella's Mother had chosen it as a gown in which she would appear at the first Ball to which she was invited.

It was therefore one in which she was to make a good impression.

It was white, as was expected of a *débutante*, and trimmed round the hem with small white roses and green leaves.

There were silver ribbons crossing over her

breast, the ends of which cascaded down the back of the gown.

"You looks lovely!" Mrs. Peel said in a tone of genuine admiration. "An' I've something to put in your hair."

"What is that?" Odella asked.

"Some white roses exactly the same as those which decorate your skirt," Mrs. Peel replied, "only they're real, an' they've got a lovely scent."

She pinned them to the back of Odella's golden hair.

Just as she had finished, there was a knock on the door.

Mrs. Peel opened it.

" 'Is Lordship's compliments," Watkins said, "but he thinks Miss Wayne might like to wear th' pearl necklace an' bracelet which 'is Mother wore when 'er was a girl."

Odella heard what was being said.

When the velvet Jewel-Box was brought to her and she opened it, she gave a cry of delight.

The pearls, which were perfectly matched, were threaded with a small diamond between each one.

The same applied to the bracelet which Mrs. Peel fastened to her left wrist.

"Now you'll hold your own with any of the ladies that's been invited to Carlton House!" Mrs. Peel said with satisfaction.

"I doubt that!" Odella answered, thinking of Lady Georgina. "But it was very kind of His Lordship, and I shall not feel so countrified, now that I am wearing this beautiful jewellery."

"There'll be plenty of gentlemen ready to tell you what you do look like," Mrs. Peel remarked. "I'd be surprised if even His Royal Highness isn't amongst them!"

Her words made Odella feel a little more sure of herself.

She went downstairs to where the Marquis was waiting for her in the Drawing-Room.

It was a large, exquisitely furnished room.

The chandeliers were lit, and as Odella came into the room the Marquis thought she might be the Spirit of Spring.

She walked towards him and saw that he was not only exceedingly smart, but there were decorations on his cut-away evening-coat.

As she reached him, she said nervously:

"I . . . I hope I . . . look all right . . . and you will not be . . . ashamed of me."

"You look very beautiful," the Marquis replied quietly, "and exactly as I wanted you to look."

Odella smiled at him and he felt as if the sun had come out.

"Now, let us go in to dinner," he said. "I do not want to be late."

"Is it . . . going to be a very . . . big party?" Odella asked as they sat down in the well-proportioned Dining-Room.

There were lighted candles on the table, which made the diamonds in Odella's necklace glitter.

"Only about a hundred and fifty to two hundred," the Marquis replied. "This is one of His Royal Highness's smaller parties. The larger ones are overwhelming. But they are given in the Summer when the Prince Regent can use the lawns, painted terraces, and waterfalls."

"I have read about them," Odella said, "but I

never thought I would be . . . able to . . . see them."

"To-night you will see all the treasures he has inside the house, which he is continually re-arranging."

"Why does he do that?" Odella asked.

"He is always buying new things, or producing them from the attics so that they can be displayed for his guests to admire."

Odella laughed.

"It sounds fun!"

"It is for him," the Marquis said, "and you will be able to enjoy them to-night. His friends never know what to expect next."

He made it all sound very light and glamorous

But when they were in the carriage going towards Carlton House, Odella said in a low voice:

"You have not . . . yet told . . . me what you expect to happen. How do you . . . think the Frenchman . . . if he is there . . . will try to . . . kill His Royal Highness?"

"I think," the Marquis said quietly, "that he will use a stiletto because it is easier to conceal about his person."

The Marquis felt Odella sitting beside him give a little shiver, and he went on:

"A stiletto is very fine and sharp, and if it passes swiftly into the heart, it is usually a minute or two before the victim succumbs. That gives the assailant time to get away."

"And . . . suppose I do not . . . remember what his . . . voice sounds like?" Odella asked in a whisper.

The Marquis reached out and took her hand in his.

"You are not to be nervous," he said. "Everything we think of, say, do, or hear, passes into our brain, which is like a store-chamber. We can never forget it, nor erase it."

"You . . . mean that . . . the way the . . . Frenchman spoke is recorded in my . . . brain . . . and I cannot . . . forget it?"

"It would be impossible for you to do so," the Marquis said. "It is there, and even if you tell yourself you will never think of it again, it is still in your mind, chronicled for eternity."

He realised Odella understood as another woman might not have done.

Then she asked:

"What shall I . . . do? How shall I tell . . . you if I . . . think he is . . . the man in the . . . darkened carriage?"

"I have arranged," the Marquis said, "that the Prince Regent will receive his guests in a narrow room which will not be crowded. The only people with him will be his two Secretaries, who will both be armed, and the General in charge of the troops that guard him by day and by night."

He paused before he added:

"And of course you and I will be there."

"Will not . . . people think that is . . . very strange?" Odella asked.

"I doubt if they will think about it," the Marquis replied, "for the same reason that each guest will be announced by one door, cross the room to where His Royal Highness is standing, then leave by another door which will lead them into the main Reception Rooms."

"I see what you mean," Odella said slowly.

"His Royal Highness will speak longer to anyone with a French name so that you will have time to hear them answer. If you recognise the voice, do not speak, just touch my arm or my hand as I am standing beside you."

His fingers tightened on hers as he said:

"Now we both have to trust in Fate, or perhaps you would say God, that we do not make a mistake."

"I have been ... praying all the ... evening," Odella said simply. "I cannot believe that ... God would allow that ... wicked Bonaparte to win such ... a victory."

"That is what we both believe," the Marquis said, "and I am certain that your prayers will be heard."

He felt Odella's fingers tremble in his.

He told himself once again that he would have done anything in his power to save her from having to go through this ordeal.

But he knew that more important than either of them was the fact that Englishmen were still fighting vigorously against Napoleon.

Although the news from the battlefronts grew more encouraging every day, it would be a mistake to relax until the French were utterly and completely defeated.

The carriage turned into Pall Mall.

The Marquis could hear the Bands of the Guards playing in the courtyard of Carlton House.

They were beneath the fine Corinthian Portico designed by Henry Holland.

The Marquis released Odella's hand knowing that she was looking about her eagerly.

Despite her anxiety, she was feeling really excited at seeing Carlton House.

It had been described by a great number of people as being more impressive than the Palaces in Russia.

They entered the Hall with its Ionic columns of brown Siena marble.

Odella felt as thrilled as if she were going to one of the children's parties which had been a delight when she was young.

She and the Marquis were received by members of the Prince Regent's household.

There were several other guests arriving at the same time.

Odella was aware that the Marquis had deliberately arranged to come early.

She noticed the respect with which he was treated.

They were taken up to a room on the First Floor.

She could see at a glance that it was beautifully and expensively furnished.

As they entered the narrow room which the Marquis had described, a Major Domo announced the Marquis's name and her own in a stentorian voice.

There was the Prince Regent himself.

He was wearing the uniform of a Field-Marshal and also the glittering Star of the Order of the Garter.

He was now fifty-one years old, but Odella thought he looked as if he might have been older.

He was still handsome, though somewhat overblown and extremely fat.

As she curtsied before him she realised, as so many other people had done, that his charm was irresistible.

His manner was most gracious and courteous.

"I am delighted to meet you, Miss Wayne," he said, "and my good friend the Marquis has told me how extremely clever you are, and how grateful we must all be to you."

Odella blushed.

At the same time, she thanked His Royal Highness for what he had said.

Her composure and manner, the Marquis thought, might have been that of a woman twice her age.

"I believe you are interested in pictures," the Prince Regent was saying, "and I hope I may have time this evening to show you some of mine."

"I would like that above everything, Sire," Odella answered, "and I believe your Royal Highness's French furniture exceeds any other collection ever seen in England."

The Prince Regent was delighted.

It always pleased him when people showed a genuine interest in his possessions.

He would have gone into a long explanation of how he had obtained the furniture after the Revolution.

But somebody else was announced at that moment by the Major Domo.

This meant that the Marquis and Odella moved to stand on one side of him.

The Colonel and the General stood on the other side.

There were two other gentlemen in the room, ostensibly attendants.

But they had a military air about them which told Odella that they were His Royal Highness's guards.

Now the guests were arriving one after another.

After the Prince Regent had said a few words to each of them, they left the room through the opposite door.

Odella had her breath taken away by the Ladies' jewellery and the richness of their gowns.

It seemed as if everybody who came to Carlton House were responding to the challenge of the splendour of the house itself.

Odella longed to look at the pictures on the walls and the furniture, of which there was a great deal in so small a room.

But she knew she had to concentrate on watching each person as they appeared.

As the names were announced, she knew that these could not possibly be the assassin for whom they were looking.

She recognised many of the names because she had read them in the Court Circulars of *The Times* and *The Morning Post*.

There was the Duchess of Devonshire wearing the most fantastic diamonds.

The Duchess of Portland emulated her with sapphires that gleamed in an enormous tiara.

The gentlemen were not to be outdone.

The gold-embroidered coats of the Diplomats challenged the uniforms of the various Regiments.

The Politicians looked rather plain beside them, even though they wore a number of decorations.

As more and more people filed through, Odella thought excitedly that it was like a scene from an Opera or some event she had read about in a book with her Father, but never expected to be actually present when it took place.

She could not help realising that the Prince was very intelligent.

He spoke to his guests about their interests as if he were really fascinated by them personally.

One he asked about his music, another about the book he was writing, to a third he spoke of his race-horses.

To the ladies he was complimentary, telling one lovely young Duchess that she enhanced his house like a lily.

Another he compared with a piece of Dresden china.

The French guests, the *Duc* de Bourbon and the *Duc* de Berri, succeeded each other.

It was when their names were called that Odella stiffened and listened intently.

The *Comte* d'Artois was a very old man who she knew from the moment he appeared, leaning on a stick, was unlikely to be an assassin.

She listened closely to their voices to make sure she recognised the special intonation whenever it came.

Then the Major Domo announced in stentorian tones:

"Mr. Walter and Lady Georgina Langford, Your Royal Highness, accompanied by *Comte* Jean de Lisle!"

The Marquis was standing close to Odella, and she was pulsatingly aware of him.

She knew he was suddenly alert.

She thought it was because the woman he loved had just walked into the room.

Lady Georgina was looking exceptionally beautiful in a gown of brilliant red silk.

It was ornamented round the hem with crimson feathers, and also on the shoulders.

She was wearing a ruby and diamond tiara and a necklace of small rubies.

As she moved with a sinuous grace across the floor, her eyes were on the Marquis.

There was an expression in them which made Odella's heart stop beating.

Lady Georgina sank down in a deep curtsy before the Prince Regent, and he said:

"It is delightful to see you, Lady Georgina, and you are looking even more beautiful than when we last met!"

"Thank you, Sire," Lady Georgina replied. "You always make me feel so happy."

"And that is what you must be to-night," the Prince Regent said as he smiled.

Lady Georgina would have spoken to him again, but he turned to her husband.

"Nice to see you, Langford," he said. "Are you backing my horse to-morrow at Newmarket?"

"Of course, Sire," Walter Langford replied. "How could Your Royal Highness be anything but the winner of that particular race?"

"I only hope you are right," the Prince Regent answered.

The *Comte* de Lisle had been detained at the door until Lady Georgina and her husband had passed through.

Then, as he came forward, Odella saw that he was a man of well above medium height, not, she thought, very young and definitely over thirty.

At the same time, there was something strong and determined about his face.

The Prince Regent held out his hand.

"I am glad to meet you, *Comte*," he said. "I have known members of your family for a long time."

"Your Royal Highness is most gracious," the Frenchman replied, "and—"

At the first words he spoke Odella recognised his voice without a shadow of doubt.

With difficulty she suppressed a cry of horror and put out her hand towards the Marquis.

It was only a slight gesture, but the Frenchman saw it.

With a swiftness which no-one expected, he sprang forward.

He flung his left arm round Odella's throat and pulled her back against him.

Then there was a long, shining stiletto in his right hand and he pressed it against her breast.

"One step towards me," he said, "and she dies!"

chapter eight

FOR a moment everyone seemed paralysed into immobility.

Then the Marquis, looking past the *Comte* as if giving orders to someone behind him, said sharply:

"Do not shoot! I want him taken alive."

The Frenchman instinctively turned his head.

As he did so, the Marquis shot him through the temple.

The explosion from the pistol echoed round the room.

As the *Comte* staggered, the Marquis leapt forward and caught hold of Odella.

He picked her up in his arms.

Without speaking, he carried her out of the room through the door by which the other guests had left.

He did not, however, go as far as the main Reception Room.

As he knew the house well, he turned aside to a room which he thought would be unoccupied.

It was a small Ante-Room, but elegantly furnished like the rest of the house.

There was a profusion of flowers and the candles were lit.

The Marquis pushed the door shut behind him before he set Odella down gently on her feet.

He realised that she was suffering from shock, and for the moment he just looked down at her white face.

She was not trembling, but was very near to fainting.

He pulled her close to him, then very gently his lips found hers.

As he kissed her, he felt her suddenly come alive.

There was a rapture moving within her which was also moving within himself.

Because he was afraid that he might have lost her, he kissed her wildly, fiercely, and possessively.

Her whole body melted into his.

It was as if they were an indivisible part of each other.

It seemed a long time later before the Marquis raised his head and Odella said in a voice with a lilt in it:

"We . . . saved him! We . . . saved . . . him!"

"*You* saved him," the Marquis said, "but, my Darling, I might have lost you."

His lips took possession of her again.

When finally he released her, he thought it impossible that any woman could look so ecstatically happy and so unbelievably beautiful.

"I love you!" the Marquis said in a deep voice. "And I think, my Precious, that you love me."

"I do . . . love . . . you, I do!" Odella whispered. "But . . . I thought . . . as you . . . loved someone else . . . you would never . . . love me."

"I love no-one but you," the Marquis said, "and I have never been in love as I am now. I knew when that devil threatened to kill you that I could no longer live without you. How soon will you marry me?"

To his surprise, Odella looked up at him enquiringly.

"D-did you . . . really ask me to m-marry . . . you?" she stammered.

"I want you as my wife, I want you with me always, and never, never again will I allow you to be in such danger as you have just passed through."

"I . . . I cannot . . . believe it!"

As if she felt shy, she hid her face against his shoulder.

He held her very close, then he said:

"We must be married at once, because I cannot let you out of my sight."

"That . . . would be . . . wonderful!" she murmured.

Then, as she looked up at him, her eyes filled with love, she gave a little cry.

"I . . . I had forgotten . . . I am . . . in mourning."

"In mourning?" the Marquis questioned.

"I . . . I did not . . . think of it again . . . but when I was waiting for . . . you to come to . . . tea I read in the newspaper that my Uncle . . . is dead, and that Papa has now come . . . into the . . . title."

"The title?" the Marquis asked in surprise.

"My Uncle's only son was killed early in the war, and so Papa now becomes the 7th Earl of Waynehead."

The Marquis was astounded.

He had been determined to marry Odella even if she were only the daughter of an obscure, unimportant country Rector.

However, it certainly made things very much easier, as far as his relatives and his own position were concerned, that her Father should be the Earl of Waynehead.

Odella gave a little sob.

"I . . . suppose," she said despondently, "we will . . . have to . . . wait."

As she spoke, the door opened and the Prince Regent came in.

He shut the door behind him, and as he walked towards them, the Earl took his arms from around Odella.

"I have come to thank you, my boy, for saving my life," the Prince Regent said to the Marquis.

"It was entirely thanks to Odella," the Marquis replied. "She was the only person who could identify him."

"I realise that," the Prince Regent concurred, putting his hand on Odella's shoulder, "and it is difficult to know how I can thank you."

"I am only so very thankful, Sire," Odella said, "that I was . . . able to . . . recognise the *Comte's* . . . voice."

"I can now proceed with my party without any more anxiety," the Prince Regent said. "But I think, Midhurst, that as I came into the room, you were expressing yourself more eloquently than I am able to do."

"I was asking Odella to marry me," the Marquis replied. "But we have a problem which I would beg Your Royal Highness with your usual skill to solve for us."

"Of course, of course, I will do my best," the Prince Regent answered.

The Prince Regent was unable for many years to take a prominent part in ruling the country.

Because of this, the Marquis knew he was always delighted when his friends and his Ministers sought his advice.

"Odella has told me, Sire," the Marquis said, "that her Uncle, the Earl of Waynehead, has just died, and her Father has come into the title. She will therefore be in mourning for some months."

The Prince Regent was listening intently, and now he said:

"I saw in today's newspapers that Waynehead had died, and of course his son was killed some years ago."

"You are always so well informed, Sire," the Marquis responded.

"As Papa now has some importance in Society," Odella murmured, "I suppose I shall have to . . . wait for at least . . . six months before I can . . . be married."

She looked despairingly at the Marquis.

He knew that she was longing to be married no less ardently than he was.

"Well, of course I have a solution!" the Prince Regent said triumphantly. "You shall be married immediately, before anybody connects you with your Uncle's death. And of course you yourself have been too pre-occupied to-day to have had time to read the newspapers."

Both the Marquis and Odella stared at him, and the Prince went on:

"The Archbishop is here. He was the next guest to arrive after you left me. I will go now and speak to him. He can marry you in my Chapel and I will, of course, give the Bride away."

"Do you really mean that, Sire?" the Marquis enquired.

"Leave everything to me," the Prince Regent replied.

He walked towards the door in a jaunty way which told the Marquis he was enjoying himself.

Nothing fascinated His Royal Highness more than an intrigue, or a love-affair which he could stage-manage.

As the door shut behind him, the Marquis opened his arms.

Odella ran towards him with the swiftness of a bird in flight.

"Is it . . . really . . . possible that . . . we can be . . . married . . . soon?" she asked.

"That is exactly what His Royal Highness is arranging now, and all I want to do is to kiss you and tell you I love you."

"And . . . that is . . . what I want . . . too," Odella whispered.

It seemed to her as if the Prince Regent had waved a magic wand.

Before anyone in the party was aware that anything unusual was happening, Odella and the Marquis were walking towards the Chapel with the

Prince Regent leading the way.

Behind them came his two Secretaries, who were the only other people who had been informed.

The Chapel, though small, was well designed.

Under His Royal Highness's direction, several exquisitely carved pews had recently been installed.

There were large solid candlesticks which came from an ancient Church, and a cross on the altar embellished with precious stones.

The Archbishop was waiting for them.

First the Marquis went ahead to stand at the foot of the steps leading to the altar.

Then the Prince Regent offered Odella his arm.

He walked up the short aisle, moving with the same solemnity he would have shown had this been Westminster Abbey.

The Service was a short one.

The Archbishop, however, conducted it with a sincerity which made Odella feel that every word he spoke was part of the Divine.

As she and the Marquis knelt for the blessing, she was sure the angels were singing above them.

As they rose to their feet, the Archbishop said:

"You may kiss the Bride."

It was a very gentle kiss, but Odella was aware that the Marquis vowed without words to keep the promises he had made.

She knew that his heart was hers for all eternity.

As they walked from the Chapel, the Prince Regent said:

"Congratulations, Midhurst, and may I wish you both every happiness. Now I must attend to my guests."

"But first, Your Royal Highness, I want to

thank you," the Marquis said, "for making me the happiest man in the world."

"And me the happiest woman!" Odella joined in.

The Prince Regent stopped suddenly.

"I was considering while you were being married," he said, "what I could give you as a wedding-present. You have saved my life. Therefore I think it appropriate, Midhurst, that you should receive a Dukedom. Your wife will certainly be the most beautiful Duchess a man has ever known."

For a moment the Marquis was too astounded to speak, and the Prince Regent went on:

"My personal present to you will be the Order of the Garter. It is what Wellington has already, and I think it only right that you should have it too."

It was impossible for the Marquis to express in words what he wanted to say.

Indeed, he went down on one knee and kissed the Prince Regent's hand.

Odella then sank down in a deep curtsy.

"Now," the Prince Regent said in a different tone of voice, "let us enjoy ourselves. We will have Supper immediately, as I want to drink your health in Champagne."

He went ahead when he had finished speaking, and the Marquis and Odella followed him.

When they reached the main Reception Room, it was to find it filled with guests all chattering excitedly about the drama that had just taken place.

Every trace of the attempted assassination had been swept away.

The only noticeable effect on the guests had been that some of them had had to be detained before they could be presented.

The Prince Regent gave his orders.

Instead of waiting as was usual until long after midnight, supper was at once brought to the tables.

They were arranged not only in the Dining-Room, but also in the magnificent Conservatory.

It was here that Odella found herself sitting on His Royal Highness's right with the Marquis beside her.

On his left was Lady Hertford, of whom he was still enamoured.

The Marquis would have preferred to keep their marriage secret.

But the Prince Regent insisted on telling everybody that it had taken place.

Odella thought his reasoning was very logical.

It was that since she had been instrumental in disclosing his assassin, she might now be in danger from other spies who would wish to take their revenge.

"The new Marchioness will be safe with her husband, whose war record is known to us all," he said. "And seeing how lovely she is, you will understand that he wants her with him by day and—by night."

He said all this in a speech which made all those listening laugh.

Then, while Odella and the Marquis remained seated, everyone, including His Royal Highness, rose to drink their health.

To Odella, it was an unbelievable enchantment that seemed like a dream.

As one delicious course followed another, she had no idea what she was eating.

She knew only that the Marquis was beside her and his vibrations joined with hers.

She felt as if their love encompassed them with a brilliant light.

When Supper was finished, the guests were informed that there was gambling in one room, and music in another.

However, because of the drama of the attempt on the Prince's life, it seemed that all they wanted to do was to chatter to one another.

It was then the Marquis said to the Prince Regent:

"I feel sure Your Royal Highness will understand that I must now take my *wife* home."

He accentuated the word "wife," and the Prince Regent smiled.

"She is enchanting—absolutely enchanting!" he exclaimed. "Run along, both of you, and if you can spare the time, Midhurst, come and see me to-morrow."

"We will do that, Sire," the Marquis said, "and thank you, thank you from the bottom of my heart."

As Odella rose from her curtsy, the Prince Regent kissed her.

"If your husband looks after you," he said, "mind you, look after him. We need men like him in this country, not only in war, but also when there is peace."

"I promise I will take great care of him, Sire," Odella said, smiling.

They went from the room but found it difficult to reach the Hall.

So many people wanted to congratulate them.

They also paid so many compliments to the Marquis on his achievements in battle, and to Odella on her looks, that when they got away she said:

"If we stayed there any longer, we should become very conceited!"

"There is plenty of excuse for your doing so," the Marquis replied.

Odella laughed.

A servant came with her wrap and put it round her shoulders.

Another servant then informed the Marquis that his carriage was at the door.

To Odella's surprise, the servants and some of the guests pelted them with rose-petals.

They hurried into the carriage, and as it drove off she said:

"Now I really feel married. I should have missed the rose-petals if people had not remembered them."

"I can remember only that you are my wife," the Marquis replied.

As he spoke he pulled her against him to kiss her.

*   *   *

Odella waited in the big four-poster bed for the connecting door into the *Boudoir* to open.

She had not realised before that the Marquis's bedroom was on the other side of it.

She thought now that he had deliberately put her there so that she was near him.

She gave a fleeting thought to the unhappiness

and misery she had felt when she thought he loved Lady Georgina.

But because she was so aware of his feelings, she knew that after to-night he would never want to think about Lady Georgina again.

Whether or not she had known that the Frenchman staying in her house was a would-be assassin, she and her husband had been instrumental in bringing him to Carlton House.

Odella did not know much about the Social World.

Yet she had the idea that, without saying anything, the ladies would draw their skirts to one side when Lady Georgina appeared.

Invitations to Balls and parties would no longer be forthcoming.

She would take no part in them as she had before.

Whatever the Marquis might have thought about Lady Georgina in the past, Odella knew now that it was she he loved.

There was no reason for her to be jealous of anybody.

"He loves . . . me! He . . . loves me!" she whispered.

Even as she did so, the communicating door opened.

The Marquis came in and because she was so excited to see him, Odella flung out her arms.

He sat down on the side of the bed and, taking her hands in his, he kissed first one, then the other.

"How is it possible," he asked, "that you can be so lovely and, at the same time, so clever? And now you are mine!"

"That is . . . what I want . . . to be," Odella murmured.

"You *are* mine," the Marquis said, "and you will never be afraid again, or risk your precious self in any wild drama in which you should not have been involved in the first place."

"It was an adventure, a crusade, and we won the victory!" Odella said.

She thought the Marquis was going to kiss her.

Instead, he took off his robe and got into bed.

He pulled her gently against him and said:

"My Darling, my Sweet. I love you with my heart, my soul, and also with my body. But I am afraid of hurting or frightening you."

Odella gave a little laugh that was like the song of the birds.

"How could you frighten me," she asked, "when I know that our love is perfect and Divine? When you kiss me . . . I feel I am . . . touching the stars."

It was then the Marquis kissed her.

He knew she had spoken the truth.

He could feel the ecstasy she was experiencing seeping through her.

It communicated itself to him until they were flying together in the sky.

It was a rapture he had never known before.

When he made Odella his, they touched the peaks of ecstasy.

Then they were enveloped with the spirit of love which comes from God and exists in a Heaven made specially for lovers.

ABOUT THE AUTHOR

Barbara Cartland, the world's most famous romantic novelist, who is also an historian, playwright, lecturer, political speaker and television personality, has now written over 590 books and sold over six hundred and twenty million copies all over the world.

She has also had many historical works published and has written four autobiographies as well as the biographies of her mother and that of her brother, Ronald Cartland, who was the first Member of Parliament to be killed in the last war. This book has a preface by Sir Winston Churchill and has just been republished with an introduction by Sir Arthur Bryant.

Love at the Helm, a novel written with the help and inspiration of the late Earl Mountbatten of Burma,

Great Uncle of His Royal Highness, The Prince of Wales, is being sold for the Mountbatten Memorial Trust.

She has broken the world record for the last sixteen years by writing an average of twenty-three books a year. In the *Guinness Book of World Records* she is listed as the world's top-selling author.

Miss Cartland in 1987 sang an Album of Love Songs with the Royal Philharmonic Orchestra.

In private life Barbara Cartland, who is a Dame of the Order of St. John of Jerusalem and Chairman of the St. John Council in Hertfordshire, has fought for better conditions and salaries for Midwives and Nurses.

She championed the cause for the Elderly in 1956, invoking a Government Enquiry into the "Housing Condition of Old People."

In 1962 she had the Law of England changed so that Local Authorities had to provide camps for their own Gypsies. This has meant that since then thousands and thousands of Gypsy children have been able to go to School, which they had never been able to do in the past, as their caravans were moved every twenty-four hours by the Police.

There are now fifteen camps in Hertfordshire, and Barbara Cartland has her own Romany Gypsy Camp called "Barbaraville" by the Gypsies.

Her designs "Decorating with Love" are being sold all over the U.S.A. and the National Home Fashions League made her, in 1981, "Woman of Achievement."

She is unique in that she was one and two in the Dalton list of Best Sellers, and one week had four books in the top twenty.

Barbara Cartland's book *Getting Older, Growing Younger* has been published in Great Britain and the U.S.A., and her fifth cookery book, *The Romance of Food*, is now being used by the House of Commons.

In 1984 she received at Kennedy Airport America's Bishop Wright Air Industry Award for her contribution to the development of aviation. In 1931 she and two R.A.F. Officers thought of, and carried, the first aeroplane-towed glider airmail.

During the War she was Chief Lady Welfare Officer in Bedfordshire, looking after 20,000 Servicemen and women. She thought of having a pool of Wedding Dresses at the War Office so a Service Bride could hire a gown for the day.

She bought 1,000 gowns without coupons for the A.T.S., the W.A.A.F's and the W.R.E.N.S. In 1945 Barbara Cartland received the Certificate of Merit from Eastern Command.

In 1964 Barbara Cartland founded the National Association for Health of which she is the President, as a front for all the Health Stores and for any product made as alternative medicine.

This is now a £65 million turnover a year, with one-third going in export.

In January 1968 she received *La Médeille de Vermeil de la Ville de Paris*. This is the highest award to be given in France by the City of Paris. She has sold 30 million books in France.

In March 1988 Barbara Cartland was asked by the Indian Government to open their Health Resort outside Delhi. This is almost the largest Health Resort in the world.

Barbara Cartland was received with great

enthusiasm by her fans, who feted her at a reception in the City, and she received the gift of an embossed plate from the Government.

Barbara Cartland was made a Dame of the Order of the British Empire in the 1991 New Year's Honours List by Her Majesty, The Queen, for her contribution to Literature and also for her years of work for the community.

Dame Barbara has now written 590 books, the greatest number by a British author, passing the 564 books written by John Creasey.

AWARDS

1945   Received Certificate of Merit, Eastern Command, for being Welfare Officer to 5,000 troops in Bedfordshire.

1953   Made a Commander of the Order of St. John of Jerusalem. Invested by H.R.H. The Duke of Gloucester at Buckingham Palace.

1972   Invested as Dame of Grace of the Order of St. John in London by The Lord Prior, Lord Cacia.

1981   Received "Achiever of the Year" from the National Home Furnishing Association in Colorado Springs, U.S.A., for her designs for wallpaper and fabrics.

1984   Received Bishop Wright Air Industry Award at Kennedy Airport, for inventing the aeroplane-towed Glider.

1988   Received from Monsieur Chirac, The Prime Minister, The Gold Medal of the City of Paris, at the Hotel de la Ville, Paris, for selling 25 million books and giving a lot of employment.

1991   Invested as Dame of the Order of The British Empire, by H.M. The Queen at Buckingham Palace for her contribution to Literature.